# RENOVATING THE RICHARDSONS

## VIRGINIA SMITH

HARVEST HOUSE PUBLISHERS
EUGENE, OREGON

Published in association with the Books & Such Management, 52 Mission Circle, Suite 122, PMB 170, Santa Rosa, CA 95409-5370, www.booksandsuch.com.

This is a work of fiction. Names, characters, places, and incidents are products of the author's imagination or are used fictitiously. Any resemblance to actual persons, living or dead, is entirely coincidental.

*Cover by Garborg Design Works, Savage, Minnesota*

*Cover illustration © Chris Garborg*

**RENOVATING THE RICHARDSONS**
Copyright © 2016 Virginia Smith
Published by Harvest House Publishers
Eugene, Oregon 97402
www.harvesthousepublishers.com

Library of Congress Cataloging-in-Publication Data
    Smith, Virginia, 1960-
    Renovating the Richardsons / Virginia Smith.
        pages ; cm.—(Tales from the Goose Creek B&B ; Book 2)
    ISBN 978-0-7369-6479-1 (pbk.)
    ISBN 978-0-7369-6480-7 (eBook)
    I. Title.
    PS3619.M5956R46 2016
    813'.6—dc23

        2015021177

**Printed in the United States of America**

15 16 17 18 19 20 21 22 23 24 / BP-JH / 10 9 8 7 6 5 4 3 2 1

# Chapter One

O f course he'll do it. When's the first practice?"

Al Richardson gaped at the woman before him. She looked like Millie, but his beloved wife would never agree to such an outrageous suggestion. The woman seated at Millie's dressing table with half the curlers still in her hair and a phone pressed to her ear must be an impostor.

From his perch on the corner of the mattress he ventured an interruption. "Excuse me."

She held up a finger to shush him and then used it to plug her free ear, attention focused on the conversation on the other side of the cell signal. "Thursdays and Saturdays are good." Pause. "Uh huh."

During the next pause he interjected with more volume. "You're wasting your breath."

She shot an irritated glance at his reflection in the mirror and then said in a sweet voice, "No, but I'll make sure he does by Thursday."

He got to his feet and stiffened his spine. Time for a show of the steely resolve for which he was renowned. "I won't do it—"

His gaze snagged on the reflection in her mirror. Jaw protruding, brow furrowed like a wheat field at planting time, he looked like an old bear. Their headstrong daughter used to display exactly the same expression when she was six years old and forced to clean her room.

He bit back the rest of his sentence, lest he appear childish—*and you can't make me!*

"Seven o'clock is good. He'll see you then." Millie disconnected the call and then twisted on her stool to face him. "What were you saying, dear?"

That innocent expression and round-eyed gaze would not work. Not this time. Al drew himself up to his full height to tower over her. "I will not play softball on the Fourth of July. I'm not the least bit interested in the sport, and I don't care a single bit about that ridiculous intra-county game the mayor is so keen on. After thirty-seven years of marriage, you should know that." Encouraged by her silence, he strengthened his denial. "What's more, I'll thank you not to volunteer me for anything without consulting me first. I'm certainly capable of making my own decisions, and I insist on doing so."

"Now Albert, don't get worked up. Remember your blood pressure."

The gentle reprimand irritated him. He set his teeth. "How can I forget when you mention it five times a day?"

When the last curler had been removed from her hair she stood and crossed the floor, nightgown fluttering around her knees. "I love you and I want you to stay healthy. Which is why you should participate in this community event. The fresh air will be good for you." She rose to her tiptoes to press a kiss on his cheek and then headed for the closet.

Determined not to be softened by a kiss, he whirled and followed. "What if I fall? I'm not young anymore, Millie. Old bones are brittle, you know. I could break a hip." He warmed to the theme. "Or an arm, maybe both. Then where would I be? Only two years and eleven months from retirement, and how can I use a computer keyboard with casts on both arms? I'll be forced into early retirement, and then all your plans for the B&B will be ruined."

There. Let her think about *that.* He indulged in a satisfied grimace. The plans for her precious bed and breakfast, which was already chomping through his financial investments like a herd of rabbits in a carrot patch, depended on his income until he reached thirty years of service and his pension was fully vested.

She pulled a shirt from the closet. "Goodness, you're being dramatic this morning."

"I feel the situation warrants it." He sucked in a breath and spoke in a tone that refused argument. "I will *not* play in that softball game."

"Of course not, silly." Clothing draped across her arm, she swept past him on her way to the bathroom. "You're too old."

*Huh?*

The words transported him into some sort of surreal existence where people spoke in opposites and nothing made sense. He shook his head sharply and then darted after her. "Stop."

Turning in the bathroom doorway, she aimed an inquisitive look his way. "Yes, Albert?"

"Didn't you just tell the mayor that I would be at the practice Thursday night?"

"Yes." She blinked those adorable round eyes, lashes fluttering like a schoolgirl's. Then a smile broke free and a pair of dimples punctuated her cheeks. "You're going to be the team manager. You know, take care of the equipment and help the coach with the lineup and practices and so on."

The bathroom door closed, shutting her away from view. Al stared at the chipped paint—something else that needed to be repaired in this crumbling old house—and took a moment to gather his thoughts. Not a player. A manager. He'd pace along the baseline, consult his clipboard, and tell the next batter when it was time to warm up. Probably have to wear the team T-shirt, which would make him look like a pudgy old man. On the bright side, he'd be among those in charge at one of the most anticipated events on Goose Creek's summer calendar. Second-in-command to the coach. An object of respect, and he wouldn't have to jeopardize life and limb.

The door opened and Millie emerged wearing old jeans and one of the stained button-up shirts that pretty much made up her Saturday wardrobe these days, since she spent hours working on the house. She managed to make even old work clothes look nice.

Tilting her head back, she looked him in the eye. "Well? You'll do it, won't you?"

Though he should dig in his heels and refuse on principle, the proposition did deserve consideration. That was a defining differ-ence between Al and his wife—she made decisions in a flash and then leaped feet-first into them. He preferred a measured, systematic examination of all aspects of a situation before making a commitment. And he could not do that while she looked at him with that indulgent smile hovering around her mouth.

He avoided a direct answer. "I don't understand why you felt the need to accept on my behalf. It's as if I have no say in my own affairs anymore." He drew a breath, prepared to point out the many expen-ditures inflicted on his bank account by her determination to reno-vate the Victorian eyesore they'd bought—most committed without his prior approval. She stopped him with an enchanting smile.

"Because, Albert," she explained in a reasonable tone, "if I'd asked first, you would have said no."

She left the room while he was trying to come up with an answer. No doubt the reasoning made perfect sense to her. Call it wifely logic, a thought process that husbands found incomprehensible but were subject to nonetheless.

"I might still say no," he called after her.

From the hallway Millie's voice floated back to him. "Come and have breakfast before your blood sugar dips too low."

Shaking his head, Albert did as he was told.

❄

The stools at the soda fountain inside Cardwell Drugstore were all occupied when the sleigh bells on the front door announced Al's arrival. Heads turned and then dipped in greeting. After a quick scan of the occupants, both seated at the counter and at one of the tables beyond, Al's stomach muscles released a few tightly wound knots. His nemesis, the man who had mounted a full-scale invasion of the sanctity and peace of Goose Creek's Saturday morning sanctuary, was not here. Thank the Lord.

Al acknowledged his fellow Creekers as he made his way to the table where Bill Zeigler and Pete Lawson waved him over. He settled himself in one of the two empty chairs, and Lucy Cardwell set a steaming mug of coffee on the scarred Formica in front of him.

He smiled his thanks. "Could I get some—?"

"Honey." She pulled a plastic bear-shaped bottle from the deep pocket in her apron and plunked it down beside his mug. "I know. Just don't overdo it or you'll have an episode and I'll have to cut you off."

Al set his teeth in a grimace as he drizzled a thin line of the thick, sweet stuff into his mug. The long arm of Millie reached into every nook and cranny of Goose Creek. She had agents everywhere. Stirring, he examined the cinnamon roll Bill was tackling enthusiastically. Thick and gooey, dripping with icing. Maybe he could...A glance at Lucy's forbidding expression banished the thought. Asking would only result in the embarrassment of denial in front of his fellow Creekers. With a sigh, he set down his spoon and sipped honey-flavored coffee.

Pete leaned back against the spindly metal chair and commented to the room at large, "Looks like they're about ready to start on the grass."

Everyone knew what he meant. Al's gaze strayed to the drugstore's front window, which looked out on Main Street. At the west end, hidden from his vantage point, a water tower stood sentinel over the town. Just over a month ago the mayor had awarded the task of repainting the town's landmark to a woman from Georgia. Her plan called for a mural to wrap around the tower's barrel, a work of art that would enhance Goose Creek's image. She'd hired Little Norm Pilkington, the son of a lifelong Creeker with a loud mouth and a penchant for stirring up trouble, to be her assistant. In the days since the pair began work the difference in the tower was already obvious, and they had not even started on the mural. Gone were the baby-vomit chartreuse paint and the uneven lettering, blessedly covered over with a nondescript primer gray that Al found immensely soothing.

"Wish they'd hurry," Chuck Geddes commented from his stool at the counter. "I'm itching to see it done."

"You'd best be getting you some cream for that itch, then. It's gonna be a month or so." Bill, chuckling at his own clever comment, sliced off a huge bite of cinnamon roll and shoved it in his mouth.

The door burst open, the jingle of sleigh bells announcing a new arrival. When he caught sight of the man who bounded—there was no other word to describe the near-leap with which he entered the store—Al's stomach twisted into a new mass of knots. He slumped down in the metal chair. Was it too much to ask for *one* day of peace?

"Morning, fellow Geese!"

Franklin Thacker pushed the door closed behind him with a nerve-jangling clang. Or maybe it wasn't the bells but the man himself who buffeted Al's nerves. A few half-hearted murmurs from various points in the store answered him, but not a single man met the newcomer's eye.

Oblivious, Thacker strode toward them. "I've been thinking. We need an official greeting. Like the Vulcans with *Live long and prosper*. Only it could be about geese, you know? Something like this." He stopped, planted his hands in his armpits, and began to flap his elbows, shouting, "Honk! Honk!"

Across the table, Pete's gaze settled on Al. A guilty flush warmed Al's face. Everyone blamed him for the Thacker infestation, and rightly so. After all, the man occupied the cubicle next to Al's at work, and had for several years. No one else could possibly know Thacker's obnoxious personality better than Al. And what did he do? He sold the man his house. Paved the way for the invasion. Rolled the Trojan Horse inside the city gates and opened the trap door.

It was all Millie's fault, of course, but no one blamed her. No one except Al.

*One more reason buying that Victorian eyesore was a bad idea.*

But of course he'd known that all along. Hadn't he tried to be the voice of reason? Begged her to reconsider? Pointed out the flaws in her plan of renovating the real estate disaster and opening a bed and breakfast to the point of nearly losing his sanity? If only he could somehow have communicated to her how extraordinarily annoying Thacker and his wife were, maybe she would have reconsidered the decision to sell their comfortable little home to them.

He heaved a sigh. Too late now. The bomb had exploded and all he could do was live with the fallout.

Thacker caught sight of him. He abandoned his attempt to create a Goose Creek greeting and advanced. "Bert! How's it hanging, buddy? Haven't seen you since, let's see." Thacker made a show of examining his wristwatch. "Since five o'clock yesterday." His hee-hawing laughter ended with a snort.

Al endured a thud on his back as Thacker rounded the table and claimed the empty chair. The man settled himself and then shouted toward Lucy, "How 'bout a cup of joe, you sweet thang, you?" He guffawed. "And some sugar, sugar."

The temperature in the room dropped an icy ten degrees. Bill tackled the last bite of his pastry with single-minded focus, and Pete seemed to have discovered a fascinating aspect of his fingernails. Al risked a glance toward Lucy and discovered the source of the winterlike chill in the store. If her expression were any more frigid, her lips would be in danger of shattering.

The door opened again, and the warmth of a Kentucky summer day flooded the glacial interior of Cardwell's. The sight of Mayor Jerry Selbo entering with his long-legged stride and sunny smile restored an atmosphere of breathability to the air. Lucy's lips thawed enough to mutter, "Morning, mayor," in a tone that approached her normally cheerful greeting. A collective breath was exhaled.

"Morning, everyone." He flashed a smile around the room and made his way past the counter to the table beside Al's. "I've just come from the Rightmiers' place. Wilma is designing the logo for our team shirts. It's looking good."

Lucy emerged from behind the counter with two steaming mugs. She placed the first in front of Jerry with a gracious nod and plunked the second down before Thacker so hard coffee sloshed over the rim.

"Oops." She made a swipe at the spillage with the dish towel she kept thrown over her shoulder before returning to her perch.

Bill twisted around in his chair to face the mayor. "So how many players we got now?"

"Only six." Jerry lifted the mug to his lips and blew the steam away. "But I'm still making calls."

"Wish I could help you out." Thacker rose, crossed to the counter, and picked up the sugar dispenser. "I'd be out there with the rest of the flock if I didn't have a trick knee. Could I have a spoon, honey bun?"

The last was directed at Lucy, who maintained a glacial glare while she plucked a spoon from the silverware bin and plopped it in front of him.

"That's a shame." Jerry shook his head. "We need all the help we can get."

Al examined the mayor closely. He sounded completely sincere. Did he not recognize the bullet he'd dodged? If Thacker joined the Goose Creek softball team, Creekers would stay away in droves.

Jerry met his eye over the rim of his mug and his smile widened. "But we do have a team manager." He lifted his coffee in Al's direction. "Right, Al?"

Suddenly the focus of attention, Al shifted in the hard chair.

"Hey, good for you, Al." Bill leaned forward to slap his shoulder.

Shaking his head, Al raised his hands. "Hold up a minute. I haven't agreed to do it."

Jerry's smile faded. "You haven't? But Millie told me you would."

"I said I'd think about it." Al shut his mouth before adding that his wife did not have the authority to volunteer him.

"You ought to do it, Al," Pete said. "I wish I could get involved, but business at the hardware store picks up in summer. I don't have time."

"Hey!" Thacker straightened, a bright gaze circling the room. "I'll be the manager. That way I can help out and my trick knee won't get in the way."

A moment of dead silence met his suggestion. Though Al dared not look directly at any of his friends, he felt the weight of several panicked gazes.

Jerry tilted his head, considering. "Well, if Al doesn't want to…"

Beneath the table, a shoe stomped on Al's foot. He opened his mouth to protest, but then he was caught in Bill's direct, round-eyed stare. The man's expression clearly said, *Do something before it's too late.*

His stomach sank. He was the one who'd inflicted Thacker on Goose Creek. It was his civic duty to minimize the damage.

"I'll do it," he told the mayor.

❄

Millie grasped a dangling corner of the hideous paisley wallpaper between her thumb and two fingers and pulled upward at an angle. A foot-long section of multicolored flowers and sprawling vines peeled away from the plaster. She raised her voice to shout over the sound of the steamer's motor. "There's something satisfying about stripping wallpaper, don't you think?"

Violet, her best friend and former next-door neighbor, passed the steamer's pan across the wall with a circular motion. "When it's all gone and the wall's got a fresh coat of paint, that'll be satisfying."

"Yes, but there's something about peeling off the old to get ready for the new." Millie scraped the bare plaster to wipe off the sticky glue left behind and then cleaned the scraper with a cloth.

"Out with the old, in with the new, eh?" Violet tilted her head and considered the wall. "I used to peel the skin off Byron's back when he got sunburn. It's the same sort of thing."

Though Millie didn't consider the two actions remotely similar, she merely muttered a noncommittal, "Hmm." To her, ridding this bedroom of several layers of decades-old wallpaper—and whoever hung paper without going to the effort of first removing the previous layer should be shot, in her opinion—was akin to spring cleaning, when the accumulation of winter's dust and dirt was scrubbed away in preparation for the spotlight that summer's sunshine would bring. The process itself was restorative. Since Violet rarely bothered with deep cleaning of any sort, the comparison would be lost on her.

The scent of clean laundry filled the room. One of the ladies at church had relayed the tip of using fabric softener to loosen the old paper instead of the more expensive commercial solutions. Another had suggested vinegar, but the idea of that odor permeating the house wasn't appealing. Fabric softener not only made the entire house smell nice, but it worked well, especially since Millie gave up trying to strip by hand and bought the steamer. Al had groused about the expense until she pointed out the cost of renting the equipment for the number of days required to remove decades' worth of wallpaper in the entire six-bedroom house. She'd saved a lot of money with the purchase.

Of course, she hadn't yet told him the cost of three dozen antique glass doorknobs. But those were a necessary purchase. The travesty of using modern doorknobs in a lovely Victorian-era house was unthinkable.

Violet finished with a section and moved sideways, taking care to pull the hot steamer hose out of the way. "When will you be able to go back to part-time at the clinic?" she shouted.

Millie stepped into the spot her friend had just vacated and tackled the paper before it had a chance to dry. "Alice Wainright starts Monday. I'll spend two days training her, and by Wednesday she should be able to handle the afternoons on her own."

For several years she'd been employed as the morning receptionist at the Goose Creek Animal Clinic, a job she enjoyed immensely. Half-days suited her perfectly. But when the former veterinarian sold the clinic last month, she'd been forced to work full time. She enjoyed working with Susan, the new vet, and she couldn't deny that the extra income had come in handy since she and Albert bought this house and began the renovation work. But between putting in a full day at the clinic and cooking supper and taking care of Albert, she had no energy to spare in the evenings. Since she staunchly refused to work on Sundays—a holdover from the old days, perhaps, but one she believed important—that left only Saturdays to focus on the house. At this rate she and Albert would be in their nineties before the bed and breakfast opened.

"Do you want me to come over Wednesday afternoon?" Violet shouted.

A satisfyingly long strip of gaudy wallpaper peeled off from the floor all the way to the height of Millie's waist. "Make it Thursday," she answered. "But come at four for tea on Wednesday."

A smile lit Violet's face beneath the helmet of hairspray-stiffened curls that remained as tight as when she arrived that morning, despite several hours' exposure to steam. "I'll bring egg salad sandwiches."

Millie rolled the sticky paper and tossed it onto the trash pile in the corner. Violet tended to be heavy-handed with the mayonnaise, resulting in egg salad that had very little taste of actual eggs. "Would you bring muffins instead? I have a new recipe I want to try. It's supposed to be healthy. No mayonnaise at all."

The next section of paper proved difficult. Millie tackled the corner with her scraper, and in doing so applied a touch more force than necessary. The metal edge gouged into the plaster, and a chunk crumbled away. "Oh, dear," she murmured. Now she'd have a hole to patch, a task she had not yet mastered. Working carefully, she slipped the edge of the scraper beneath the thick layers of wallpaper and pried upward. More plaster crumbled away. She put a finger in the hole, dismayed when a sizeable portion tumbled to the floor. The wall felt damp and almost squishy. Either the steam was penetrating all the way through the plaster, or—a sense of foreboding settled in her stomach—the dampness was coming from inside the wall.

"Violet," she called, "look here."

Her friend switched off the steamer's motor and stepped to her side. "You've poked a hole in the wall."

"Yes, but look." Millie hooked her finger inside the plaster and gave a slight tug. Another section crumbled away, leaving an opening big enough to see wood inside. Obviously very old wood, since the house was over a hundred twenty-five years old, but was old wood supposed to darken like that? The anxiety in her stomach blossomed. Using her finger, she tore at the crumbly plaster until she had uncovered a sizable section of the interior. She and Violet bent forward to look inside.

Violet straightened, shaking her head. "That wood's moldier than month-old bread."

Millie shut her eyes against the sight. Albert's attitude must be rubbing off on her. All she could see in her mind's eye was a huge, flashing dollar sign.

## Stripping Wallpaper–the DIY Method

*Items Needed:*
   Fabric softener (use the inexpensive store brand)
   Water
   Sponge
   Putty knife or scraper
   Box cutter or razor blade

Combine one part fabric softener with one part water. Using the sponge, saturate the wallpaper you wish to remove. Wait ten minutes. In the bottom corner of a panel of wallpaper, use the scraper to lift an edge of the paper, and then pull *slowly* upward and diagonally. When you've peeled off as much paper as possible, use the scraper to remove the rest. Reapply the solution if necessary. If paper is stubborn or is in layers, slash the paper with the box cutter before applying the fabric softener solution. Take care to only slash the paper and not the wall. You will need to wash the wall with clean water and may need to patch damaged areas before painting or repapering.

# Chapter Two

I'm afraid it's been leaking for quite a while. Years, by the look of it."

Justin, also known as Hinkle the Handyman, delivered the news with a sympathetic grimace. He'd interrupted his work on the B&B's roof at Millie's request and now stood in the front bedroom with her and Violet, peering at the disturbing dusty growth inside the wall.

Millie received the pronouncement with a stoic mask firmly in place. Beside her, Violet *tsk, tsk, tsked*.

They stood before a sizeable hole in the plaster that Justin had made with a hammer in an attempt to discover the extent of the mold. They had yet to find a section of unmoldy wood, which meant the damage was widespread enough to cast a cloud of worry over Millie's normally cheerful attitude.

Justin seemed to sense her concern. He forced a smile. "On the positive side, at least we found the cause. The copper pipe looks intact and in good shape. The corrosion appears to be limited to the leaking elbow joint where it comes around the top of this wall."

Millie looked where he indicated. A network of plumbing branched off and headed toward bathrooms in a couple of different directions. "Does that mean it's only this wall that's moldy?"

He hesitated, his expression cautious. "I hope so. If the damage is confined to this one pipe, then the wall in the upper floor is probably okay. But we'll need to check the room below."

"There's no arguing with gravity," Violet intoned as one delivering sage wisdom. "It will always win."

Millie bit her tongue. Normally she enjoyed Violet's endless store of quotable quotes and overused clichés, but just now she wasn't in the mood.

"The front parlor is beneath this room." Her favorite room in the house, with the beautiful bay window and ornate crown molding and the gorgeous ash hardwood floor she planned to have sanded and restored. The parlor wasn't on her list to be worked on until early next year, after this bedroom and the one with the second-best view in the back of the house.

Justin fixed a kind smile on her. "Maybe it hasn't gone all the way down. Let's hope for the best."

Violet took her hand and gave it a sympathetic squeeze. Swallowing against the lump of gloom that had lodged in her throat, Millie nodded.

A noise in the hallway alerted them to the arrival of someone else. A voice called, "Millie? Are you up here?"

Panic gripped her insides. She whirled toward Violet and grabbed her other hand. "It's Albert. What will I say?"

Albert, whose pessimism over the house was a mounting conflict against which she struggled daily, would no doubt view this setback as an omen. She'd be forced to listen to his complaints about the unanticipated expense, the incompetence of the inspector who should have detected this before they bought the house, and at least a dozen other *I told you so's*. Could she hide the hole? Alarm pinged in her brain as she cast a frantic glance around the room. Maybe one of the longer sheets of wallpaper?

"There you are." Albert sauntered in from the hallway, a small smile on his heavy features. He nodded a greeting at Violet. "You'll never guess what I agree—oh." He stopped short when he caught sight of Justin. "I thought you were working on the chimneys today."

"I am. Just lending a hand here for a minute." The young man gestured toward the giant hole in the plaster.

Albert inspected the wall, a frown gathering on his forehead. "I thought the plan for this room included removing the wallpaper and painting. Why are you tearing down a wall?" He stepped forward, bending at the waist to examine the damage.

Millie forced an even tone. "That's what we were doing, but then we found—"

"Mold!" Albert jerked upright and whirled on her. He stabbed an accusing finger at the hole. "That's mold."

Justin examined his shoes while Violet edged toward the window and became fascinated by something on the front lawn.

Mustering her courage, Millie faced her husband. "Yes, I know, but Justin has already found the cause, and it can be repaired."

"Repaired?" He drew himself stiffly upright. "Mold is deadly, Millie. Poison!" A hand waved frantically in the air between them. "We're breathing poison at this very moment!" He grabbed the collar of his polo and ducked his neck to shield his mouth and nose. "I knew this place would be the death of us."

Her patience nearly exhausted, Millie folded her arms across her chest. "Don't be so dramatic."

Justin stepped forward. "Al, I'm not a mold expert, but I'm pretty sure this isn't black mold. If you're allergic to mold it might make you sick, but I don't think it will kill you."

"That explains this headache." Al's voice was muffled by his shirt. "And the nagging cough. I haven't felt well for a month, not since we moved in."

"Now you're being ridiculous," Millie snapped. "You're not allergic to anything. I haven't heard you cough a single time, and you haven't complained of a headache."

"I've suffered in silence," came his aggrieved reply.

A ridiculous claim, not worthy of an answer. In all the years they'd been married, Millie had never known her husband to endure anything, even a hangnail, in silence.

Millie faced Justin, presenting her back to her husband. "So what's the plan? How do we determine the extent of the damage, and what can we do to fix it?"

With a quick glance at Albert, the young man cleared his throat. "I know a mold removal specialist. Want me to give him a call?"

"A specialist?" Albert repeated. "That sounds expensive."

Violet offered an appropriate cliché without turning from the window. "There's no such thing as a free lunch."

Gritting her teeth, Millie ignored them both. "Please do. Ask him to come at his earliest convenience."

"Yes, ma'am." Justin hurried from the room, obviously relieved to escape.

Millie faced Albert. "If you want to help strip the rest of this wallpaper, you're welcome to stay. Otherwise, there's a Honey-Do list on the refrigerator."

She thought he might offer further arguments, but after only a moment's hesitation he followed Justin with a long-legged stride, his shirt collar still clutched to his face.

Violet finally turned away from the window. "I'm glad that's over. The tension was so thick you could cut it with a knife."

Millie glanced gloomily at the mold-splotched wood. "If you think that was bad, wait until he gets the bill."

※

Dr. Susan Jeffries pressed her stethoscope against her patient's tiny chest. The rapid heartbeat tap-danced in her ears while bulging brown eyes watched her face. She inched the drum down and listened to the rumble of an active digestive system.

Removing the earpieces, she smiled at the Chihuahua's anxious owner. "Everything sounds good."

Nina Baker blew out the breath she'd been holding. "Thank goodness. Pepe will be ten next month, and I don't think I'd be able to handle it if..." She winced. "You know."

Standing on the metal table, Pepe shivered. It did feel a bit chilly in this exam room. Susan retrieved the sweater he'd arrived in and slipped it over his head, taking the opportunity to run her fingers down the slender legs to feel his patella. "I don't see any sign of the health problems common to this breed. Older Chihuahuas sometimes develop knee problems, but his are fine. I'll check his blood work, but I don't see any reason why Pepe shouldn't live to a ripe old age. Fifteen or even twenty is normal."

That brought a wide smile to Nina's face. "Thank you, Dr. Jeffries." She gathered her dog into her arms for a hug, and Pepe snuggled beneath her chin, obviously accustomed to the position.

"Call me Susan." She plucked a pen out of the pocket of her new lab coat and tapped on the embroidered name, *Dr. Susan.* A few weeks ago she'd decided her old lab coat, which identified her as *Dr. Jeffries,* was too impersonal. The beloved former veterinarian, from whom she'd bought the Goose Creek Animal Clinic, had been known simply as Doc. If she wanted to be accepted by the pet-owning community in this small town, she'd need to be friendly and informal. That was what Justin advised, and she agreed.

Justin. A familiar warmth flooded her. Everything reminded her of Justin these days. And how could it not, when the image of his smile was branded on her mind's eye, and the memory of his kiss burned in her heart?

"Dr. Susan it is." Nina ducked her chin toward her pet's ear and spoke in the high-pitched, indulgent tone many pet owners used. "We like her, don't we, Pepe? We'll come back and see Dr. Susan again, won't we? Say bye-bye now." She grasped a tiny paw between her fingers and waved it.

"Bye-bye, Pepe. I'll see you in six months." Susan picked up the folder and stepped around the exam table to open the door. "I don't expect the blood work to show anything, but if it does I'll give you a call."

With a happy nod, Nina snuggled her dog and preceded Susan down the hallway and through the swinging door that separated the exam area from the waiting room. After scribbling a few notes on the chart, Susan handed the folder to the weekend receptionist. Hazel Duncan, a sturdy woman with a head full of spiky brown locks, glanced at it and began pounding on the keyboard without a word, either to her or to their customer. Susan bit back a sigh. Hazel was certainly competent, if a bit forbidding. Whereas Millie, the regular receptionist, practically bubbled friendliness and neighborly goodwill. Hopefully the new afternoon receptionist would be more like Millie. If only Millie would continue to work full time. But Susan understood her desire to spend time readying her house to open her bed and breakfast. And besides, Millie's B&B was the reason Justin spent his days in Goose Creek, close enough that they could have lunch together several times a week.

Again, the thought of Justin conjured his image, and Susan allowed herself a soft smile. In a few hours she'd be on the back of Justin's motorcycle, on their way to their favorite roadside diner and a long ride through the central Kentucky countryside.

A man emerged from the kitty waiting room. "All finished for the morning?"

With a start, Susan looked into a familiar smiling face. "Daddy! What are you doing here?" The question came out sharper than she intended.

His smile faded. "I'm here to spend the weekend with my little girl. Is there something wrong with that?"

"N-no. It's just—I mean, I—" She snapped her mouth shut. Daddy's appearance on weekends had become rather more common than not in the past month. No doubt about the reason, either. He disapproved of her relationship with Justin, who'd dropped out of college after a year and worked a blue-collar job, two decisions Daddy viewed with disdain.

But today he was earlier than normal. Though most of the vice presidents at the bank where Thomas Jeffries had spent his entire professional career did not work on Saturdays, he always made it a point to be in his office whenever the bank was open. Their hometown of Paducah was four hours' drive away, and since the time was now just shy of noon, he would have had to leave early.

"Of course not. I'm surprised to see you, that's all. Did you take the day off?"

"I did more than that." He straightened his spine. "I have an announcement, one I think you'll approve of."

A tickle of discomfort erupted in Susan's stomach. How well she recognized that granite-like expression. Regardless of his words, she steeled herself against something unpleasant. "Oh?"

The rumble of wheels over tile drew their attention to Hazel, who rolled her chair forward to plant her elbows on the reception desk, an expectant gaze fixed on Daddy. In the months since Susan bought the animal clinic—with Daddy cosigning the loan, a fact she must never forget or fail to be grateful for—she'd become aware that this reception desk formed a firmly established link in the Goose Creek gossip chain. At least Millie's actions in spreading news throughout town were always goodhearted. If a client's cat was about to have kittens in need of a good home, Millie could be counted on to spread the word. Hazel's news, on the other hand, occasionally held a touch of venom.

"When is my next appointment?" Susan asked the watchful woman.

With a glance at the computer monitor, she answered, "Not for thirty minutes." She settled her chin on her hands, clearly waiting for the announcement.

Daddy lifted his classic Roman nose into the air and, with a look at Hazel, addressed Susan. "Let's talk in your office. Perhaps your secretary would be so kind as to run into town and bring us a sandwich."

Hazel stiffened in the chair, eyes snapping fire. He might as well have asked her to pick up his laundry. Susan hurried to intercede before the feisty woman, whose feminist leanings were no secret around town, could fire off a retaliating volley.

"Daddy, she's a veterinary receptionist, not my secretary." She flashed an apologetic grimace toward Hazel. "Besides, I have ham and cheese in the fridge. We'll share."

She hooked a hand around her father's arm, halting him in the act of reaching for his wallet, and dragged him through the swinging door, safely out of firing range of Hazel's sharp tongue.

In the clinic hallway, she whispered, "Please don't insult Hazel. She might quit."

He cast a disdainful glance toward the door. "Let her quit. You can replace her easily enough."

She heaved an exasperated sigh. "You have no idea how hard it is to find people who'll work for the salary I can afford to pay. Besides, Hazel has a lot of friends in this town. Business is finally starting to pick up, and I can't afford to lose a single patient."

"Don't coddle your employees, Susan. Be friendly, yes, but they need to know who's boss."

Several replies leaped to mind. This little clinic was not a bank, and she was not a vice president with a commanding presence. And while Paducah might not be a major cosmopolitan city, it was ten times the size of tiny Goose Creek.

Instead, she left his comment unanswered and retrieved her sandwich from the clinic's dorm-size refrigerator. When they were settled in her office with the door shut and her neat desk between them, she divided her sandwich and set the bigger half on a tissue in front of him.

"There." She smiled at him and picked up her lunch. "Now what's this about an announcement?"

"I've decided it's time for a change, both personally and professionally." He leaned back and crossed one leg over the other, clasped his hands, and rested them on his shin. "I've spent a lot of time thinking about this, and I'm satisfied it's the right move."

The discomfort that had begun a few moments before intensified. Susan set her untouched sandwich down. "What move is that?"

He cleared his throat. "I've decided to sell the house and move to Goose Creek."

The silence in the office served as a backdrop to a loud crash that reverberated inside Susan's mind—the sound of her love life, her relationship with Justin, shattering like a crystal bowl smashed with a sledgehammer.

※

The discovery of mold succeeded in doing something rare indeed: it dampened Millie's enthusiasm for further work on the house. After Justin returned to his project on the chimneys and the back door slammed behind Albert downstairs, she retrieved her putty knife and made a halfhearted effort to scrape the glue from the panel of wall they'd stripped before the dreadful sighting.

"This glue has dried," she announced in a despondent tone. "Would you hand me the sponge?"

Instead of picking up the bucket containing the fabric softener mixture, Violet cocked her head and peered at her. "You've had the wind knocked out of your sails."

"You're right." Millie lowered the scraper. "I knew we'd encounter difficulties along the way, of course. But mold?" She slumped against the wall and slid down to the floor.

Violet deserted the steamer hose and sat beside her. "Could be worse. At least the pipes are in good shape."

"As far as we know." The worries that she kept stuffed deep inside bubbled dangerously toward the surface. Albert was so pessimistic about this renovation project, and indeed about the whole bed and breakfast plan, that she did not dare voice anything but optimism and a positive attitude. But truthfully, she did have doubts. At the base of them, lurking like a monster in the depths of a dark, scary cavern, was the possibility that Albert's dire predictions would come true. That this house, and her bullheaded determination to renovate it, would bankrupt them.

"What if this is only the beginning?" She turned her head to look at Violet. "What if there are other leaks we don't know about?"

"Just the tip of the iceberg?" Violet asked.

Millie answered with a miserable nod. "We could end up tearing into every wall in the house. And what if Justin's wrong and it *is* black mold? We'll all die. When I get to heaven, Albert will be standing there at the pearly gates and he'll say"—Millie ducked her chin and spoke in a low voice—"'I told you buying that house was a bad idea, Millie.'"

Violet's lips twitched, but then her expression grew concerned. "You're as glum as a funeral." She climbed to her feet and held out a hand. "Come on. You need some cheering up."

Millie took her friend's hand and allowed herself to be hauled upright. "I don't feel like being cheered up. I'd rather wallow in misery for a while."

"Baloney. I'm prescribing an old-fashioned remedy for depression. Chocolate malts at Cardwell's soda fountain."

"But what about the wallpaper?" Millie gestured vaguely toward the half-finished wall.

"It'll still be there on Thursday. And besides, what if the mold specialist says we have to take out the whole wall? We'll have wasted our time peeling off the paper."

Millie scowled at her friend. "Like *that's* supposed to cheer me up?"

But oddly enough, she did feel better. Violet had the right idea. When a situation threatened to get the best of one, it was time to walk away. Time and distance helped one gain perspective.

"You change clothes," Violet instructed, "and I'll run home and do the same. I'll meet you at Cardwell's."

With a final glance at the disaster in the wall, Millie nodded. "Sounds like a plan."

She followed Violet out of the bedroom, pulling the door shut behind them.

❊

Of the dozen or so buildings that stretched down either side of the railroad track on Goose Creek's Main Street, Millie's favorite was the one housing the Freckled Frog Consignment Shop. When originally constructed a century and a half ago, the building had been home to the railroad office. Since the town was built for the sole purpose of serving and profiting from the railroad, the building received extra attention during its construction. She loved the heavy carved wooden arch that covered the entry, the decorative off-set bricks above the second floor windows, and the extra deep window wells at street level. True, the building needed a bit of attention, as did most of the original structures in town, but she agreed with Frieda, the owner, that to replace the original façade would destroy the charm of the place.

Satisfyingly full of chocolate malt, and with her attitude much improved, Millie wasn't quite ready to go home. She bid Violet farewell and crossed Main Street to pass beneath that beautiful arch into the Freckled Frog. A mishmash of colors and scents combined in a cheerful jumble on the shelves and various display cases crowded throughout the shop. Frieda's inventory, everything from handmade jewelry to scented soap to heavily ornate stained glass lampshades, could only be described as eclectic. In Millie's privately held opinion, there wasn't a practical item in the entire store, but that didn't prevent her from spending delightful hours fingering one fascinating piece after another.

A cluster of ladies gathered around the back counter called greetings as she pulled the door shut behind her.

"Hello, girls," she answered. "Beautiful day out there."

Francine Ryan fanned herself with a flapping hand. "Bit warm for my taste."

"It's your age, dear." Betty Hunsaker patted Francine's arm. "Get yourself some Black Cohosh. It'll work wonders for those hot flashes."

Several heads nodded agreement. A flash of brilliant blue caught Millie's eye and she paused to finger a crocheted scarf with half an ear toward the ladies as they continued their conversation.

"Pete got a look at the color," Cheryl Lawson said, "and it's entirely wrong. More teal than green."

"Do you think she's going for bluegrass?" asked Betty.

"If so, she needs to open her eyeballs." Frieda's biting tone spit disapproval. "Kentucky's grass is as green as anywhere else, and she'd better make it look that way."

Some unfortunate person was the object of an uncomplimentary conversation. Millie loved newsy chatter as much as the next woman, but she disliked spiteful talk. She sauntered toward them, plastered a smile on her face, and assumed her sweetest voice. "Who's on the menu for today?"

The comment drew sharp stares from Betty and Cheryl.

After a moment's uncomfortable silence, Frieda laughed. "We were discussing the water tower mural. Ms. Barnes ordered some of the paint through Pete's hardware store, and the colors are off."

Millie had not yet met Sandra Barnes, the artist hired to paint the town's iconic water tower, but from everything she'd heard so far, she approved. The woman was in a tough position. Being an outsider with such a visible and important task was sure to draw the criticism of several notoriously stiff-necked Creekers. That in itself was enough to recruit Millie to her side.

"I'd be interested in seeing them." She turned a smile on Cheryl. "Did Pete bring home color tiles?"

Cheryl didn't meet her eye. "Well, no. But he said the green was more blue than green."

Millie let a laugh ring through the store. "My Albert is the world's worst when it comes to colors. If I left the decision up to him, we'd have gold walls with black trim throughout the house." She grinned at Cheryl. "Purdue's colors, you know."

Betty agreed. "Ralph's completely colorblind. Can't tell green from orange, and that's the honest truth."

"Pete's good with color." A stubborn expression settled over Cheryl's features. "If he says the grass is going to be too blue, then somebody had better do something before we end up with another disaster."

Thankfully, Millie was saved from answering when the door opened and a woman stepped inside. No, she didn't merely step. She *swept* inside, trailing several feet of wispy leopard-print fabric behind her from the hem of her skirt. A mass of dark blonde hair roosted in an untidy knot on the top of her head, and her skin was of a darkly tanned color that spoke of long hours in the sun. From a shoulder strap swung a ragged macramé bag that might have been new twenty years ago.

She shut the door and began to browse, drawn to a pottery mug which she picked up, turned over, and set back down with a hissing intake of breath. Millie hid a grin. She and Violet shared the opinion that Frieda wanted far too much for that pottery, even if it was hand-thrown.

"Hello," Frieda called out from behind the retail counter.

"Oh!" The woman's head jerked toward them as though surprised to find she wasn't alone. Giant golden hoops dangled from her ears, and wide eyes peered through a curtain of bangs that bore a resemblance to a sheep dog's. "Hullo."

"Let me know if I can help you find anything," Frieda said.

"Thanks. I'm just looking."

Her skirt swayed hypnotically around deeply tanned calves as she wandered over to a glass-topped counter holding a display of handmade jewelry. Millie's gaze was drawn to her feet, where bright purple toenails rested on a pair of brown flip-flops almost as old as her purse. When she extended a hand to pick up a necklace, the metal clang of half a dozen bracelets jingled like bells.

The ladies did not resume their conversation, which Millie counted as a blessing. Instead, they watched the shopper while pretending not to. She *was* rather fascinating, in a hippie sort of way. Millie gauged her age at around fifty, ten years younger than she herself. She hummed as she wandered, a habit in which Millie also indulged, but only in the kitchen where no one except Albert could hear.

When the stranger ran a finger down the blue scarf, Millie broke the silence. "That's a lovely color, don't you think?"

The bracelets clanged again as she parted her bangs to peer at Millie. "It's beautifully made, too. Look at the stitches. So nice and even."

"Do you crochet?"

Gold hoops swayed as she shook her head. "No, I make candles." She turned in a complete circle, scanning the shop. "Do you have any candles?"

Frieda rounded the counter to join them. "I don't think I've ever had any consigned here."

A wide smile revealed a set of blindingly white teeth. "Well, then maybe you could sell mine. They're nothing super fancy, but they're clean-burning and I make them in a bunch of colors."

Frieda's expression became guarded. "I'd have to see them first. I'm selective about my inventory."

"Oh, sure. I'll bring you some in a couple of days. As soon as I can find them." Her bangs fluttered in the breeze of an airy laugh. "They're packed away in some box or other."

At the mention of boxes, the other ladies gave up all pretense of not listening, and openly faced the newcomer.

"Are you moving to town?" Betty asked.

The woman nodded. "I'm renting a house over on Canada Street."

The street behind the animal clinic. Millie ran down a list of possible houses in her mind. "You're renting from the Sanders?"

"I think so. I'm really awful with names." Another breezy laugh. "Which is obvious, since I haven't told you mine." She extended a hand toward Freida. "I'm Tuesday Love."

Frieda's arm halted in the act of rising, but she recovered quickly. "Tuesday Love. What an interesting name. I'm Frieda Devall."

"And I'm Millie Richardson." Millie stepped forward to shake the woman's hand next. "Were you born on a Tuesday, dear?"

Tuesday squeezed her fingers with a grip firmer than most men's. "No." She winked behind her bangs. "Tuesday was my parents' day off."

During a moment of shocked silence, Millie's cheeks warmed. "I see. Um. Well, welcome to Goose Creek."

"Thank you." Tuesday moved toward the others, who peered through goggle-eyes as she shook their hands one after another, chatting the whole time. "I'm not just moving to town. I'm setting up shop here too. Right over there." She pointed out the window toward the north end of Main Street.

"You're renting the building across the street?" Cheryl asked.

"Nope." Tuesday flashed a huge grin. "I bought it. I'm here to stay."

Frieda's eyes narrowed to suspicious slits. "What kind of shop are you setting up?"

"Oh, honey, don't worry." The woman wrapped an arm around Frieda's shoulders and squeezed. "I'm not the competition. I'm a massage therapist."

Millie would have laughed at the others' stunned expressions if she weren't so surprised herself. "You give massages? You mean, like..." She wiggled her fingers in the air.

"Oh, there's a lot more to massage than that," Tuesday assured her. "And I also do nails." She extended a foot to display her shiny purple toenails. "Just polish, though, organic and completely natural. None of that fake stuff, on account of its being poison for your nail beds."

Millie risked a quick sideways glance at Betty, who was inspecting her inch-long acrylic nails with a horrified expression.

Noticing, Tuesday covered her mouth. "Oops. Sorry, honey. After

I get set up, why don't you come by my place? I can get those offa there for you and give you something to help restore the damage. Anyway, I've got to run. I hope all y'all visit me when I open. And spread the word. Toodles."

With a farewell wave and a flutter of fabric, she swept across the store and exited into the bright June sunshine. The door shut behind her, leaving them open-mouthed.

Millie recovered first. "I had no idea that building had been sold."

"Pete hasn't said a word about it." Cheryl bit a lip. "Maybe it's just me, but I'm not sure I like the idea of a massage place in Goose Creek."

"It's not just you." Betty pursed her lips into a disapproving line. "This is a family-oriented town. We don't want that kind of business here."

Though she needed time to consider the idea, Millie wasn't ready to pronounce judgment on Tuesday Love yet. "Now, girls, let's be fair. That building has been vacant for years. If she bought it, Goose Creek has already benefited. And new business is good for the town."

"Not *that* kind of business." Frieda shook her head with such vehemence her glasses slid sideways on her nose. "A massage parlor on Main Street? It'll give the town a bad name."

Ever ready to defend the underdog, Millie fixed a reproving glance on Frieda. "You sound like she's opening a brothel. She's a massage *therapist,* for heaven's sake. You have to be licensed to do that." A thread of doubt crept in. She really had no experience from which to speak, only a vague impression. "Don't you?"

"I don't care one bit about her license." Cheryl folded her arms across her chest with a jerk. "If I catch Pete within a hundred yards of the place, he'll be sleeping on the couch for a year."

While the others voiced agreement, Millie remained silent. An uneasy tug-of-war took place in her mind. Being a business owner herself—which she would be, if they ever managed to get the house in decent enough shape for guests—she felt an affinity for anyone with enough vision and fortitude to launch a business. Especially a lone woman well beyond the vitality and energy of youth. On the other hand, how would she feel if Albert announced one Saturday morning that instead of going down to Cardwell's to hang out with the guys, he thought he'd head over to Tuesday Love's place for a massage?

*I know exactly how I'd feel.*

Good thing their house had six bedrooms, because Albert would need one.

# Chapter Three

I'll have the tilapia," Susan told the server.

They'd been seated at an out-of-the way table in the rear corner of Malone's, an upscale restaurant in Lexington. Quiet music played from hidden speakers, and soft lighting cast the dining room in a warm glow. If she and Justin were here alone, she would have enjoyed the atmosphere immensely. Their date sidetracked, they'd been forced to abandon their plans for an evening alone.

Seated to her right, Daddy scrutinized the menu like it was a loan application. There had been nothing else she could do except invite him to come along. She couldn't very well leave him sitting alone in a hotel, could she? At the mention of burgers at the roadside diner where they'd planned to go, he'd insisted on selecting a restaurant in Lexington, one with a "decent menu."

The server scribbled Susan's order and then turned to Justin.

"The sirloin, medium-rare, a loaded baked potato, and add on the salad bar please." He handed over the menu with one of the grins that Susan found so endearing.

The woman smiled back—women always smiled at Justin, a fact that caused Susan no amount of private agony—and then cast an inquisitive look across the table.

Disapproval flowed in nearly palpable waves over the top of

Daddy's menu toward Justin, who stirred his raspberry lemonade with a straw and pretended not to notice. The unspoken judgment on Justin's dinner selection grated on Susan's nerves. What did it matter to him that Justin had a hearty appetite? The man worked hard at a physically demanding job all day long. If he wanted a large meal in the evening, he deserved it. Heaven knew he didn't suffer from the extra calories. A warm glow settled in her stomach, and she resolutely refused to glance at the muscular arms and trim waist that hovered in her thoughts far more than she cared to admit.

In an act of solidarity in the face of Daddy's unspoken censure, Susan looked up at the server. "A salad sounds good. Could you add that to my dinner as well?"

Daddy's jaw and menu snapped shut at the same moment. "Baked chicken," he managed to grind out. "Rice. Steamed broccoli." He glanced toward Justin's glass, lips a tight line. "And I'll stick with water."

The moment the server moved out of earshot, he leaned forward. "Susan, those salad bars are a petri dish for bacteria. You know that." His expression hardened as his gaze flickered toward Justin. "Or you used to."

"Some probably are, sir," Justin agreed. "But I bussed tables at this restaurant one summer when I was working construction. They're careful, and their kitchen is cleaner than most families'. The food inspectors always give this place a perfect score." He met Daddy's glare with a pleasant smile, and then rose and rested a hand on the back of Susan's chair. "You hungry?"

"Starved."

Without looking toward her father, Susan allowed Justin to help her stand up. They wound their way through the restaurant's dining room toward an immense salad bar, where she picked up a chilled plate and eyed the display. She rarely ate buffet-style food, having heard Daddy's warnings about the unhealthy practices of restaurant staffs her whole life. But everything here looked fresh; the lettuce was crisp, the cherry tomatoes were ripe-red, and the salad dressings were kept chilled in deep wells of ice.

"I'm sorry our date got sidetracked," she said while arranging a bed of lettuce on her plate. "I was looking forward to the ride and a burger."

He shrugged. "This place is great. Just different."

The cucumber looked as if it had been sliced only moments before. She placed a few on her plate. "When Daddy showed up at the clinic today, I couldn't believe it. And especially with his announcement."

"Really?" His shoulders heaved with a silent laugh. "I expected it."

"You did?"

"Well, him showing up today, anyway." He halted in the act of sprinkling olives on his salad and turned to look her square in the eye. "He's been here every Saturday night for a month."

She lowered her gaze. "I know. He's trying to sabotage our..." The word *romance* stuck on the tip of her tongue. Their romance was still too new to talk about in those terms. "Our relationship."

"I know." Justin reached beneath the glass canopy protecting the food and scooped a spoonful of shredded cheese. "You're his child, and he's protective of you. I'd probably be exactly the same if my only daughter started dating a flunky who rides a motorcycle and pounds nails for a living."

With her free hand, Susan grabbed his arm. "You're not a flunky. You're a successful business owner who works harder than anyone else I know. There's nothing wrong with pounding nails." A flush warmed her cheeks. "And I like your motorcycle. A lot."

That hypnotic grin appeared. "I love it when you defend me." His eyes sought hers, and his whisper became a private caress. "You have nothing to worry about, Suz. The only person who can drive me away is you."

Suz. No one had ever given her a nickname before.

The path back to the table might have been lined with clouds, so light were her feet.

Daddy stared with unconcealed disdain at the mound of food on Justin's plate. "If I ate all that, I wouldn't be hungry for three days."

Smiling, Justin unrolled his silverware and laid the napkin across his lap. "I burn a lot of energy in my job, sir."

"Hm."

Susan speared a lettuce leaf, aware of her father's critical stare at her modest salad. She ought to be hungry, since she'd been unable to eat her half sandwich after their discussion this afternoon. But the tension around the table worked on her appetite, and she had to force herself to take a bite.

Justin had no problem, and ate with a carefree attitude she envied.

"So," he said between bites, "Susan told me you're planning to move to Goose Creek."

Daddy didn't answer at first, his distaste at discussing his plans with Justin apparent in his scowl. Eventually he gave a curt nod.

"I'll bet your bank won't be happy to see you go." Justin took a roll from the basket in the center of the table. "You're a big man down there, aren't you?"

"I'm an officer," he conceded. "I'm confident I can convince the board that the Lexington branch will be a good base for an executive to work from. If not, I'll find a similar position nearby."

"There isn't a bank in Goose Creek," Susan told him.

He shrugged. "The drive here this evening was only forty minutes. I understand a lot of people who live in Goose Creek commute to Lexington."

Justin nodded. "That's true. But I'm surprised you'd want to live in such a small town. It'll probably be easier to find a place to live here in Lexington."

Daddy's spine stiffened. "The decision is made. I'm moving to Goose Creek where I can"—he glanced at Susan—"help Susan with the animal clinic. After all, I have a vested interest in making the business successful."

The comment fooled no one. Daddy might have been interested

in keeping an eye on his investment, but mostly he wanted to keep an eye on his daughter. She slumped in her chair. If Daddy moved to town, she'd never have a free moment again.

How Justin managed to maintain his casual tone, she couldn't imagine. "She seems pretty capable to me. She knows her stuff, and she's got a good head on her shoulders."

"Of course she does," Daddy snapped. "She's my daughter." His chest inflated, and his battle to maintain his composure showed plainly on his face. When he continued, it was in a calmer tone. "But it will be a while before the animal clinic shows a significant profit. And she can't go on living in that garage apartment. I plan to buy a house somewhere in town that has enough room for both of us."

Susan's fork clattered to her plate. She turned a disbelieving stare on her father. "You want me to move in with you?"

"It's a financially sound arrangement. The money you save on rent will enable you to get our business on solid ground faster." He glanced at something over her shoulder. "Our dinner has arrived."

While the server set plates of steaming food in front of them, Susan risked a look at Justin. For once, even his pleasant demeanor had slipped. He stared at his steak like it had once been a treasured pet.

Daddy, on the other hand, had become positively cheerful. "My chicken looks delicious," he told the server. "Thank you for delivering it so promptly."

Though her fish did look good, Susan couldn't force herself to eat a single bite.

❋

Millie hovered at the top of the basement stairs, waiting for the mold specialist to emerge. Her fingernails carved deep crescents in her palms, and she forced her hands to unclench. Violet, seated behind her at the kitchen table, munched on a lemonade cookie. Though Millie appreciated her friend's support while the mold man performed his inspection, today Violet's habit of slurping her tea set Millie's teeth on edge.

"How long has he been down there?" She glanced at the clock on the kitchen wall. "Seems like hours."

"Good things come to those who wait." Violet waved a half-eaten cookie in the air and offered another quote. "No news is good news."

Over the past ninety minutes, Millie had been treated to what seemed like hundreds of clichés. Her patience nearly gone, she drew in a breath before replying in a more-or-less conversational tone. "You said that one before."

"Some are worth repeating." Violet dunked the cookie in her tea-cup and then popped it in her mouth.

The cell phone resting on the kitchen counter began playing "Fixer-Upper," a song she'd found amusing when her young grand-daughter first recommended it. Apparently her sense of humor had become moldy, like everything else around here, for she found her-self gritting her teeth.

The display identified the call as coming from the Goose Creek Animal Clinic. "It's work," she announced and snatched the phone up. "Hello, Alice. Is everything okay?"

Poor Alice had expected to spend at least two full days training with Millie. Her panicky expression when her trainer rushed out to meet the mold man after only two hours had pricked Millie's con-science all afternoon.

"I hope so?" The hesitant voice ended in an upward tone that turned the answer into a question. "Mrs. Barnes paid cash and she only had two twenties? I didn't have any change? So we owe her four dollars?"

Drat. She'd trained Alice on the credit card reader and told her to put the checks in the safe before she left for the afternoon. Almost no one paid with cash these days, but elderly Mrs. Barnes refused to use a card or even checks. Millie kept the petty cash in a locked cashbox, and she'd forgotten to tell Alice where she kept the key.

"Didn't Susan know where the keys to the cashbox are?"

Alice's voice lowered to an awed whisper. "I didn't want to bother *her*."

Though they'd only had a couple of hours together, one thing had become plain when Alice spoke of her previous job. Her boss had been a harsh woman with a razor-sharp tongue and a ready supply of more foul words than Violet had clichés. It would take time for poor Alice to lose her fear of making a mistake, even though Susan was one of the sweetest people Millie knew.

Millie poured assurance into her tone. "Don't worry about it. Just put a sticky note in the cashbox and we'll take care of it tomorrow. The key is in the desk drawer beneath the extra paper clips." The sound of heavy boots clomping up the stairs rose from below. "Alice, I've got to go. Call back if you need anything else."

She disconnected the call and hurried across the room to the basement doorway.

A serious-faced man with heavy features, Larry Nestor, who Millie couldn't help thinking of as merely Mold Man, wore a frown that sent her heart plunging toward her feet. The news must be terrible for him to scowl like that.

Before the man could speak, the back door opened. In walked the last person Millie expected—or wanted—to see at this moment.

"Albert! What are you doing home so early?"

If there was bad news to be heard, she'd much rather hear it alone. Then she could take a few hours to decide the best way to present it to her pessimistic husband.

He tossed his keys onto the counter. "I skipped the staff meeting so I could hear the verdict."

He crossed the kitchen in a couple of steps, arm extended toward Mold Man. The two exchanged names while tension stretched the knots in Millie's stomach almost to the point of nausea.

Larry shook his head. "Wish I had better news. That leak's been active for a while. The lathe's moldy all the way down to the basement, and it's growing on the studs as well."

"Stuff's thicker than fleas on a hound dog," murmured Violet.

Millie shot her a poisonous glare. Her friend ducked her head and fell silent.

"I figured as much." Albert shoved his hands in his pockets. "What do we do about it?"

Momentarily shocked out of her panic, Millie stared at her husband. No exclamation? No bemoaning the verdict? No "I told you so"? He was certainly handling the news better than she. Maybe that was a benefit of a perpetually pessimistic attitude. When disaster struck, it enabled one to take things in stride.

"We're gonna hafta rip out the lathe. C'mere and I'll show you."

Mold Man and Albert left the kitchen, with Millie and Violet hurrying after. They followed him to the parlor, where a hole had been knocked in the plaster directly beneath the one in the bedroom above. Inside was a wall made of horizontal, narrow strips of wood that looked something like window blinds. At the familiar sight of mold covering the wood, a hot, sick churning began in the pit of Millie's stomach.

"First you're gonna have to bust out all this plaster." Mold Man made a wide gesture indicating the entire wall from floor to ceiling. "Then all this lathe is gonna have to come out."

The whole wall? A small groan escaped Millie's tight throat.

Lips pursed, Albert's head bobbed in a nod. "What about the wall studs?"

"I didn't see anything to indicate structural damage, but we'll know more once we get in there."

Violet patted Millie's arm. "That's good news, anyway."

No cliché, thank the Lord. Millie managed a weak smile.

"We'll treat the wood to kill the mold, which'll take a couple of days at the most, and then you can have the walls rebuilt."

Only a few days?

"Well that's not so bad," Millie said.

"For *this* wall," Albert replied in an ominous tone. He addressed Larry. "Is there any way to tell if there's more mold without ripping out every wall in the house?"

"Sure is. We've got infrared cameras to detect leaks behind walls and ceilings. We can do surface swabs in every room, and when we've cleaned this area we'll take air samples to test for airborne mold spores." Mold Man flashed a comforting smile toward Millie. "If there's any more mold in this house, we'll find it."

Violet gave her arm another pat. "This house will be clean as a whistle before you know it."

The outcome did sound more hopeful than she'd anticipated. Still, there was one question that had yet to be asked. Millie couldn't bring herself to ask it, but of course, Albert did.

His glower deepened. "How much is all this going to cost?"

Larry shrugged. "No way to know until we get in there and see what we're dealing with."

"What about insurance?" Albert asked.

"Insurance?" Millie perked up. She'd completely forgotten about insurance. "Will our insurance cover this?"

Larry sucked in his cheeks. "Depends on your policy, I guess. Most don't unless the mold is a result of an accident."

"I'll call and find out," Millie said. "Maybe our policy is one that will."

The look Albert gave her told her exactly what he thought of that idea. Her brief surge of hope burst, and the prickle of tears stung her eyes.

He must have seen how close she was to crying. Albert was not given to public displays of affection, but he placed an arm around her shoulders before asking in a resigned voice, "When can you get started?"

The show of kindness nearly sent her over the edge. Blinking hard, she followed Albert and Mold Man to the door, listening with half an ear as they arranged the schedule for work to begin. Their voices grew distant as they headed down the hallway.

Alone with Violet, she sank onto the window seat. "I wish I hadn't insisted that Susan hire an afternoon receptionist. Looks like I'm going to need the extra money."

Her friend sat beside her, uncharacteristically quiet. She patted Millie's leg. "Maybe this will be the only mold in the house."

"Maybe."

Another long span of silence followed, and then Violet leaned sideways to nudge her with a shoulder. "Stop frowning. You don't want your face to get stuck like that, do you?"

That elicited a small smile. "I used to say that to the kids when they pouted."

"Did it make them stop?"

"No." The memory of a teenage Alison rolling her eyes rose in her mind.

Violet shrugged. "Now you know how they felt. Pretty lame advice when you're down in the dumps, huh?"

The comment struck her as funny, and she started to chuckle.

"That's more like the Millie I know." Her friend patted her leg. "Besides, this isn't all bad. You wanted to repaint this room anyway. We'll just do it sooner than we expected. And somebody else is gonna strip the wallpaper for us."

She sucked in a deep breath and blew it out, banishing gloom as she did. It was not in her nature to wallow in pessimism. That's one reason the Good Lord put her and Albert together, so her optimism could counter his glass-half-empty attitude. Maintaining a cheerful demeanor was her wifely duty.

She turned on the seat. "You're right. Everything's going to work out. Every cloud has a silver lining."

A wistful expression settled on Violet's face. "I wish I'd said that."

Millie laughed, feeling freer than a moment before. "Let's go finish our tea." She hooked her arm through her friend's and headed for the kitchen.

# Millie's Lemonade Cookies

¾ cup powdered sugar

⅔ cup butter, room temperature

2 oz. cream cheese, room temperature

Juice from one large lemon

Zest from one large lemon, divided

1 tsp vanilla

4 tsp frozen lemonade concentrate, thawed and
   undiluted

2 cups all-purpose flour

½ tsp salt

### Lemon Glaze

2 cups powdered sugar

½ tsp lemon zest

3 Tbsp frozen lemonade concentrate, thawed and
   undiluted

⅓ cup cream

Preheat oven to 325°. Line a cookie sheet with parchment paper. Using an electric mixer, combine butter and cream cheese until creamy. Add ½ cup powdered sugar and continue beating. One at a time, add lemon juice, lemon zest (reserving ½ teaspoon zest for the glaze), vanilla, lemonade concentrate, and salt. When that mixture is completely combined, gradually add flour. Beat until just combined. Dough will be crumbly. Using a spoon, form 1-inch balls and press them into discs. Cookies will not rise or expand—these will be solid, crumbly lemon cookies. Place them 1 inch apart on the paper-lined cookie sheet. Bake in oven for 20-25 minutes, until bottoms are browned and cookies are cooked through. Remove and cool on cookie sheet for 2 minutes.

Whisk ingredients for the glaze until smooth. Dip the top
of each cookie in the glaze, and then let the cookies sit until
the glaze is set. Store in a sealed container. Makes approxi-
mately 36 cookies.

# Chapter Four

On Thursday evening after an early supper, Al and Millie loaded Rufus in the car and headed out to the first softball practice.

The town of Goose Creek did not own a softball field. Mayor Selbo had somehow convinced Junior Watson to move his cantankerous old bull out of his front pasture and had paid some local kids to clean the area and construct a makeshift ball field.

Al pulled off the side of the Watsons' gravel driveway to park behind a long line of cars.

"Goodness, it looks like the whole town is here." Millie didn't turn from the passenger window. "I'm glad I thought to bring a chair. Pop the trunk, please."

Al did as he was told, trying to ignore the nervous tension that had plagued him all day whenever he thought of tonight's practice. What was he doing here, an old man in his sixties? He should be at home, puttering in his yard and watching the birds flock to his feeders.

Only his yard was a field of weeds, and his birdfeeders had been overtaken by squirrels. And his *real* yard, the one he'd worked so hard on, was now owned by Franklin Thacker.

Resolutely, he extracted the folding chair from the trunk and followed Millie down the gravel driveway to the place where a long line of chairs and blankets had been spread along the fence so the crowd could watch the practice. A much smaller group stood inside the fence.

Millie selected a place and instructed him to set her chair beside Violet's while she led Rufus away to speak to her boss, who was seated beside a distinguished-looking older man. Must be the veterinarian's father, the one Millie disliked.

Al offered a greeting to Millie's friend as he unfolded the chair. "Hello there."

Violet eyed him coldly. "Don't 'hello there' me. I'm not speaking to you."

Though he could have pointed out the obvious, her attitude piqued his curiosity. "What have I done?"

With a quick glance around their immediate area, she whispered, "You moved *them* in next door."

No question concerning the identity of *them*. But the accusation was completely unfair.

"I did no such thing. Selling the house to the Thackers was Millie's idea."

"She didn't know what she was doing." Her eyes narrowed. "You knew *exactly* how annoying they are, and you sold your house to them anyway."

In his sixty-two years Al had made plenty of mistakes for which he would accept full responsibility. This was not one of them. He drew himself up. "I refuse to take the blame for Thacker." Curious, he cocked his head. "What's he done, anyway?"

She gave an offended sniff. "He calls me Plum."

"Well, he calls me Bert," Al pointed out.

"After he leaves for work in the morning, Lulu opens every window in the house and screeches at the top of her lungs."

Al scratched his head. "Screeches?"

"She calls it singing practice." Violet shuddered. "Apparently she's taking lessons. And you should see what he's done to the backyard."

Alarm shot through him like a lightning bolt. "My backyard? What—"

"Al! Over here!" Jerry Selbo stood amid the group inside the fence, waving in Al's direction. He cupped his hands around his mouth. "Time to get started."

Al looked down at Violet. "We'll talk about this later."

"Hmph!" She turned pointedly away.

Forcing thoughts of his beautiful yard on Mulberry Avenue from his mind, Al located the gate and joined the group standing around a chalked X on the ground.

Jerry welcomed him with a smile and a clap on the back. "Here's our manager."

"Welcome, manager!"

A familiar voice grated on Al's ears as a figure shuffled into view. What was Thacker doing here?

"I thought you had a bad knee." Al worked hard to keep his tone neutral, which was probably a wasted effort. Thacker never seemed to know when he wasn't wanted, no matter how obvious the message.

"Doesn't mean I can't help." The man held up an electronic tablet. "I've been working on a program to analyze each player's strengths and weaknesses."

With an effort, Al managed not to roll his eyes.

Jerry addressed the group. "I think we can get started. Here you go, Al." The mayor thrust a spiral notebook into Al's hands. "Let's get a list of the players and their phone numbers. Tonight we'll decide who's playing which positions, and then we'll practice hitting and catching."

Junior, wearing worn denim overalls with no shirt, piped up. "I'm the shortstop on account of I'm letting y'all use my field."

Junior Watson as shortstop? The fastest he ever moved was when the supper bell rang. Al raised an eyebrow and caught Jerry's eye.

"That's our agreement," the mayor admitted. Then his expression grew stern. "As long as you do a good job, Junior. If we find out you're

better in another position, we'll move you for the good of the team."
He raised his voice and addressed the assembled. "I expect we'll shuf-
fle around a bit until we see what we've got to work with."

Al freed the pencil from inside the spiral, recorded Junior's name,
and wrote *shortstop* beside it. Good thing it wasn't an ink pen, and the
eraser looked new.

Jerry continued. "We only have eight practices between now and
the Fourth of July, so it's important that we all be here for every one."

When Norman Pilkington elbowed his way between Junior and
Little Norm, Al nearly dropped his pencil. What was he doing here?
The man had to be in his seventies.

"We-el," he drawled, "'at there might be a problem onct or twict. I
got me a farm to run. And since m'boy spends s'much time up at that
water tower"—he cocked his head to glare at Little Norm—"me and
Eulie's havin' to do everythin' ourselves."

"Pa, you oughtn't to be playing anyway," Little Norm said. "You
might get hurt."

"Pshaw!" Norman's thick gray eyebrows dropped down in a scowl.
"Been playin' ball m' whole life." He pounded his right fist into a
cracked, ancient ball glove that Al suspected had not been used since
the 1920s.

The rumble of an approaching motorcycle interrupted what might
have become an argument.

"Oh, good." Relief flooded Jerry's voice.

"Hinkle is on our team?" Al asked. Maybe they'd actually have a
chance with a strong young man like him.

"I wish." Jerry shook his head, regret plain on his face. "The rules
say only residents of Goose Creek can play. But he played baseball in
high school, so he's going to help me coach."

"Sorry I'm late," Justin announced as he hurried through the gate.
"What did I miss?"

"We're just getting started." Jerry looked over his team. "Okay,
here's what we have so far. Fred's our catcher."

Al recorded Fred Rightmier's name and position. Before the next practice he'd find a clipboard somewhere.

Thacker, hovering behind Jerry, said, "Spell your last name for me, Fred."

While Fred did, Thacker tapped on his tablet. Al felt himself beginning to bristle. Was the annoying man trying to usurp his responsibilities? Then again, Thacker was merely collecting data for his program, which was a ridiculous idea that would probably go nowhere.

Jerry continued. "Paul, can you handle centerfield?" Paul Simpson nodded, and Jerry waited for Al to finish writing and Thacker to finish tapping. "Little Norm is going to pitch, and Chuck will play second base."

As Al scribbled, Thacker sidled over to him. "I'll get everybody's names from you tomorrow at work, okay Bert?"

Gritting his teeth, Al nodded.

Norman stomped toward Jerry and stood directly in front of him. "How 'bout me? Where you gonna put me?"

Jerry rubbed a hand across his mouth, clearly hesitant. "I'm thinking right field."

Though Al knew little about baseball, he did know enough to recognize that right field saw the least activity of any position. Norman's scowl deepened, and he opened his mouth to protest, but Justin spoke before he could.

"I hope you've got a strong arm, sir. Whoever plays right field has to get the ball all the way in to third base, the longest throw in the game."

Norman's mouth snapped shut and his chest puffed. "I c'n handle it."

Jerry cast a grateful glance at Justin. "Good. Sharon's going to be in left field."

Surprised, Al eyed Sharon Geddes, who stood beside her husband. He'd assumed she was there to support Chuck. What a chauvinistic assumption. In many ways, Al really was the dinosaur Millie accused him of being. He recorded Sharon's name in his notebook.

"I'll play first base," Jerry said. "But we still need a third baseman."

Justin scrubbed a hand through his hair. "What about some high school kids? Surely there are some good athletes in town we could recruit."

A good suggestion. Al could think of several teenagers who would virtually guarantee they had a winning team.

But Jerry shook his head. "The rules state that the players have to be eighteen years old."

"Who came up with these rules?" Al asked.

"I met with Sheriff Grimes and Fitzgerald, the Morleyville mayor, a week or so ago." Jerry glanced around their small team. "We need to do some recruiting. A third of our team has to be women or we'll take a five run penalty."

"Five runs?" Justin gave a low whistle.

Norman pounded his ancient glove. "Eulie'll play if'n I tell 'er to. Want me to fetch 'er?"

All heads turned toward the observers. Al located Eulie, looking frail in her folding chair beside Sandra Barnes, the big, rawboned painter from Georgia.

Little Norm turned a stern glare on his father. "Not a chance, Pa."

For a moment Al thought Norman would argue, but Justin interrupted. "Let's ask for volunteers." The young man strode to the fence and addressed the watchers in a voice loud enough to be heard from one end of the line to the other. "We want to thank you all for coming out to support us at our first practice. As you can see"—he half-turned to wave in the direction of the small group clustered around home plate—"we need a few more players to fill out our team. Anybody out there interested in playing softball?"

Al scanned the crowd. Where were all the young men? Surely Goose Creek boasted a few young men among its residents who wanted to play softball. But if so, there were none present. At this rate, the softball game promised to be a fiasco. What was the mayor thinking when he signed Goose Creek up for a public debacle?

Al cast Millie a why-did-you-get-me-into-this glance, but she was chatting with Violet and probably couldn't see his expression from this distance anyway.

※

Susan sipped from her water bottle and battled irritation at the nearly palpable disdain radiating in Justin's direction from her father. Daddy had been completely charming to everyone, the amiable bank professional with a wide smile and easy manner, until Justin's motorcycle appeared. Now he sat in the camp chair with his arms folded and legs crossed, his lips twisted into a distasteful smirk.

Justin paced the fence line, scanning the crowd. "All right, folks. I know there are some ball players out there. C'mon and join the fun." He stopped directly in front of her. "And by the way, this is a coed team. I'm sure Mrs. Geddes isn't the only lady in town who wants to play."

He looked directly at her, and his gaze pinned Susan to her chair. Surely he didn't mean *her*?

"My mommy can do it!"

A childish shout came from somewhere to her left. When Justin looked in that direction, Susan let out a pent-up breath.

"Hush now, Willow," answered a familiar voice. "I don't play softball."

Susan twisted in her seat and caught sight of Alice Wainright seated on a quilt with her four children spread out around her. Thick, unruly mops of dark hair topped each small head, though Alice's locks were light brown and spaghetti-straight.

"Yes you do, Mom." A boy who looked to be around nine jumped to his feet and shouted toward Justin. "She plays baseball with me and Forest all'a time. She's a fair batter, but she can catch anything."

An edge of panic crept into Alice's voice. "Be quiet, Heath. That's just backyard play with you kids."

Daddy leaned toward Susan. "Isn't that your new afternoon receptionist?"

Susan nodded.

"She's too mousy to be a ball player."

The comment jabbed at Susan's already raw nerves. She shot Daddy a reproving scowl.

"Alice!" Justin called toward the woman, who looked horrified to find herself the object of attention. "Is it true you can catch a baseball?"

"I—I guess so," she admitted.

"Sure she can." The other boy, who must have been Forest, grabbed Alice's arm and tried to tug her off the quilt. "Do it, Mom."

"Yeah, Mommy." Seven-year-old Willow put a skinny arm around the youngest child. "I'll watch Tansy while you play."

A commotion stirred the crowd when Millie left her chair and approached the family. "Don't worry about the children, Alice. I'll keep an eye on them."

When she plopped down on the quilt and pulled Tansy into her lap, several in the area called encouragement.

"Go on, Alice."

"You can do it."

Finally, and with clear reluctance, Alice got to her feet and headed for the field amid cheers. Susan twisted around in her chair to find Justin staring at her.

"We still need at least one more woman."

No doubt about it. He meant her. Blood drained from her face, leaving her lightheaded. Mouth dry, the only answer she could manage was a slight shake of her head.

"It'll be fun." His appealing grin appeared. "We'll get to spend every Thursday and Saturday together for the next month."

Someone behind her called, "Honey, if I was twenty years younger, that'd do it for me."

Laughter met the comment, while Susan fixed Justin with a wide-eyed stare.

*Don't do this to me. Please, don't!*

Beside her, Daddy snapped a response in her defense. "Don't be ridiculous, young man. Susan is a professional."

The words slapped at her. Stinging, she turned toward her father. "What do you mean? Just because a person holds a professional career doesn't mean they're incapable of doing anything else."

He gave her a paternalistic smile and patted her arm. "Sweetheart, you ran track in high school for a reason, remember? Stick to what you're good at."

Part of her brain acknowledged the truth of his words. Since the time in second grade when she lost three teeth after being hit square in the face with a soccer ball, she'd avoided any sport that involved a ball. She could outrun any kid on the field or court, but whenever she saw a ball speeding toward her, she had only one instinct—duck.

But her arm burned from the condescending pat. Daddy didn't fool her one bit. His only goal was to keep her as far from Justin as he could.

Before she was more than half-aware of her actions, she was on her feet. "I'll do it."

❄

Al recorded the veterinarian's name in his notebook as she left her chair and approached, her feet dragging. For a moment when Millie stood, he feared she'd been about to volunteer. Thank goodness he wasn't put in the position of trying to talk sense into her in front of half the town.

Thacker, with his finger hovering over his tablet, directed a question to Jerry. "What position are these girlies going to play?"

Sharon fixed him with a narrow-eyed glare. "They're women, not girlies."

Oblivious as usual, Thacker nodded vaguely. "So what positions?"

Jerry contemplated his team. "Tell you what. Let's practice a bit of catching first before we decide."

"Good idea." Justin sketched an imaginary line with his finger. "Line up there, and Little Norm and I will throw."

They started to move, and Jerry called, "There's some extra gloves in that tote over there if you didn't bring one."

When everyone stood in the line, Al took up a position to one side. What was the manager supposed to do during practice?

Thacker bounded up beside him. "Let me see your roster, Bert. I'll update the names in my database."

Swallowing a wave of annoyance, Al held his notebook out for Thacker's inspection. Curious in spite of himself, Al asked, "What's your program supposed to do, anyway?"

"It'll evaluate the players' performance and identify their strengths and weaknesses. I've built an algorithm to analyze the data I input over the next few practices." His thumbs tapped with impressive speed.

Al looked up in time to see Little Norm execute an underhanded toss to Susan, who shut her eyes and cringed. The ball bounced off her foot.

"Seems to me their weaknesses are going to be pretty obvious," Al commented drily.

"Oh, Bert, you'll be surprised at what comes out of this program." Thacker entered the final name and grinned at him. "It'll be good stuff, I *garr-own-tee*." He hee-hawed, ending in the nerve-grinding snort that Al heard from the other side of his cubicle wall all day long.

Catching practice lasted thirty minutes. As her boys had asserted, Alice caught every ball, even the overhanded pitches that Justin started lobbing her way. To Al's surprise, Norman didn't miss a single ball. Hard to tell from where he stood, but it did appear that Little Norm's pitches to his father lacked the intensity of the others.

Thacker took careful notes. What data was he entering? And more importantly, was he doing something the manager should be doing? Al strained his neck to see, but the tablet's screen couldn't be read from the side.

"I think that's good for now." Jerry stepped out of the catching line. "Let's practice some hitting. Al, you want to get the bats ready?"

At the mention of his name, Al perked up. Finally, something to do. He located a pile of softball bats and lined them out on the ground in order of weight while Justin organized the team.

"Little Norm, you're on the mound." He pointed to the chalk X in the center of the makeshift infield. "Alice, I'd like you over by third until your turn to bat. Junior, you cover second."

Junior's mouth drew into a pout. "I'm the shortstop."

"I know. This is only for batting practice." Justin smiled until the pout disappeared and Junior headed for his assigned position. "And Chuck, let's put you there near first."

The rest of the team lined up along the baseline between third and home. First up was Susan, who approached Al like she was heading for the firing squad. She studied the bats a moment and then lifted a helpless expression to him. "I have no idea what I'm doing."

Her confession stirred pity in Al. Poor girl.

"Neither do I," he confided in a low voice. He retrieved the lightest bat. "Why don't you give this one a try?"

Fred, his face protected by a catcher's mask, hovered behind the X that indicated home plate. Jerry came to stand beside Al while Justin guided Susan to the batter's position with an arm around her shoulder.

He backed away. "Okay, let's see your stance."

From where he stood Al couldn't see her expression, but from the way Justin's face softened, her terror must have been obvious. He moved her a step closer to the X and arranged her hands on the bat.

"Place your feet apart," he instructed. "Now hold the bat up here like this." He placed her arms in the proper position and then stepped back to inspect her. "There. That's your stance. Does it feel comfortable?"

Though she faced the other way, her shrill answer carried on the evening air. "Are you kidding? Of course it's not comfortable."

Al exchanged a glance with Jerry. Would this ballgame result in a lover's quarrel? Seemed likely at this point.

Justin's eyebrows rose slightly, but his smile stayed in place. "It will eventually. Now, watch the ball. When it gets about here"—he leaped in front of her and held a fist in the air—"swing at it." He shouted to Little Norm. "Nice and slow, okay?"

Little Norm nodded, adjusted his footing, and tossed a slow, underhanded pitch. The ball passed by Susan, who never moved, and thudded solidly into Fred's glove.

Justin's expression did not change. "You have to keep your eyes open, Suz. Otherwise you won't be able to see the ball."

"I know that," she snapped. Then her voice took on a fearful wail. "But what if it hits me?"

"I promise you, it's not going to hit you." He pointed to the pitcher. "See Little Norm out there? He's way too good to hit a batter. Come on, let's try it again."

Fred threw the ball back to Little Norm, who caught it deftly. The second pitch was as accurate as the first, and this time Susan swung. The ball sailed past her.

"Okay, that was better. A second too early, but not bad. Let's try another one." He called toward the pitcher, "Just like that."

During the next six attempts, anxious tension gathered in the air around the pasture. Al glanced at the watching crowd. Even from the distance, he could see Millie's taut frame and worried expression. Violet perched on the edge of her chair, hands clasped in front of her mouth as if in prayer. Susan's father sat with his arms folded across his chest, his tight-lipped scowl clearly visible.

As the ninth pitch sailed through the air, the mayor drew in an audible breath. Though Al detected no difference in Susan's swing, she finally connected with a satisfying crack when the ball met wood. A cheer rose from the crowd and from the team. Al and Jerry exchanged relieved smiles.

Susan stood frozen as the ball sailed through the air for a few yards and then rolled toward third base.

"Run!" Justin shouted, grinning and giving her a gentle shove.

She did. Alice dashed forward and scooped up the ball. She made eye contact with Chuck, who stood near first base with his glove ready. For a few heartbeats nothing happened, and Al looked from Alice to Susan, still clutching the bat as she dashed toward first with impressive speed. Not until she'd almost arrived did Alice throw the ball, a strong pitch directly to Chuck, who caught it and turned to tag Susan...too late. She sailed past the base mark amid cheers and applause. The grin she turned on Justin held enough triumph to light a stadium.

He cupped his hands around his mouth. "Great job. Now come on back." He addressed the rest of the team. "We'll run the bases later. For now, let's just practice hitting. Okay with you, coach?"

Jerry splayed his hands. "Fine with me."

The next player in line, Norman, shuffled over to the bats. He picked up three, testing the balance of each and gazing down its length like inspecting a pool cue before finally selecting one. Al made a note beside his name, recording his selection. Apparently he was going to be the bat boy as well as the manager, and that was okay by him. The last thing he wanted was to stand there looking like a useless appendage. Like Thacker. Al glanced behind him to find Thacker's thumbs drumming on his tablet.

With a nod at Justin, Norman took his stance. "Come on, sonny," he called toward the pitcher. "Gimme a good 'un and watch 'er fly."

The difference between this pitch and the previous ones was obvious to even Al's untrained eye. The ball sped toward the batter box, and Fred hunched down, catcher's mitt poised to receive it. But to Al's surprise, Norman's swing connected. The ball soared into the air, heading toward third base. More cheers erupted from the watchers.

Norman dropped his bat and took off—well, it couldn't exactly be called running. He half-jogged, half-sauntered down the baseline with his odd bowlegged gait. He hadn't taken four steps before Alice raced backward, watching the ball's arc, and nabbed it out of the air.

"Looks like we have our third baseman," Jerry commented to Al. "Or third basewoman."

Any answer Al might have made died on his lips as he watched Norman, who turned his head to watch Alice catch his fly ball and promptly tripped over his own feet. Down he went, to an audible gasp from the crowd. He landed with a thud, rolled onto his back, and began yelling with more volume than Al would have thought a man his age could produce. Everyone on the field raced toward him, Justin arriving a second before Little Norm.

"Twisted my dadburned ankle," he moaned as Al approached. "On account of this dadburned uneven ground, and a dadburned clump of grass."

"Lie still, Pa," commanded Little Norm. "Let me see if it's broken."

"It ain't broke," his father snapped. "I've had broke bones afore, and I know what they feel like. This'un's just sprained."

Eulie arrived, along with several of her friends. She stood over her husband. "What've you gone and done now? Didn't I say you was too old to go running around bases with the young folks?"

Justin looked up from his inspection of Norman's ankle. "I don't think it's broken, but a doctor needs to take a look at him. Somebody want to call an ambulance?"

Norman erupted, jerking up to a sitting position. "I ain't ridin' in no dadburned ambulance."

"I'll take him."

Little Norm stooped down to slip a strong arm around his father's waist while Jerry supported him from the other side. Moving slowly, they got him upright. The fact that he could walk, albeit leaning heavily on his son and cursing the *dadburned* everything, was a good indication that the ankle was, indeed, only sprained. Safely loaded in Little Norm's pickup, the team and onlookers watched as they pulled down the gravel drive and turned onto the road.

Jerry folded one arm across his middle, propped his elbow, and rubbed his fingers across his mouth. "I guess I have some more calls to make. Looks like we're down a player."

"Be nice to have some reserve players," Justin commented.

A flash of guilt attacked Al. Should he offer to play? No, he'd end up like Norman, being hauled off the field and taken to the hospital. And if by some miracle he managed to escape injury, he would only humiliate himself. The veterinarian was a better player than him.

# Chapter Five

Jerry's hand tightened on the receiver, and he worked to keep his tone even. "I know that, Theo, but at this point I don't have a choice. Either I play, or we can't field a team."

A chuckle sounded through the phone. "Having a rough time getting volunteers, are you? Not surprised. You don't have much of a pool to draw from over there."

Teeth clenched, Jerry drew in a quiet breath. Goose Creek was roughly half the size of Morleyville, a fact that its mayor, Theo Fitzgerald, loved to point out at the county mayoral meetings.

"We had a man injured last night. One of our best players."

"Norman Pilkington is one of your best players?" Now the chuckle became an open guffaw. "This game is going to be more fun than I thought."

Jerry rocked forward in his chair, spine stiffening. How did Theo know what happened at their first practice? One of last night's onlookers must have connections in the enemy camp. They had a spy on their hands.

Voice still infused with amusement, Theo said, "If you can't even scrounge up nine players, maybe you want to go ahead and forfeit."

Jerry chose to ignore the comment and answered only when he was certain no hint of irritation would sound in his voice. "There's nothing that says the coach can't play too, is there?"

"Heck, we *made* the rules. You know there isn't."

"Fine. That's all I wanted to know." He managed to eek out a fairly polite, "Talk to you later, Theo," before pressing the button to disconnect the call. He replaced the receiver and slumped in his chair. The field chart spread out on his desk contained eight penciled-in names. The half-dozen calls he'd made this morning had garnered nothing except six polite but firm, "Thanks, but no thanks." Where was that famous all-American love of baseball? Was he the only Goose Creek resident who wanted to uphold their town's honor?

His gaze slid toward the telephone. Okay, so maybe this game represented something a bit more than a friendly game between towns. If he could once—just once—wipe that arrogant smirk off of Theo Fitzgerald's face.

Though it pained him, he picked up the pencil and wrote his own name on the line above the X representing first base.

The door opened and his secretary stuck her head into his office. "You'd better hightail it over to the water tower. There's a ruckus about to start."

Jerry dropped his head onto his hands. "Of course there is. Because today wasn't bad enough already."

Sally gave him a sympathetic pat on the shoulder as he passed her on his way out.

The water tower stood at the south end of Main Street, a three-minute walk from city hall. Four spindly legs rose one hundred thirty feet into the air, its bucket-shaped barrel topped with a pointed dome that Jerry privately thought resembled a dunce cap. When the repainting was completed, the tower would become a Goose Creek icon, an artistic representation of the quaint and tranquil town. At least, that's what he hoped. Over the past few months the tower had been a source of turmoil and civic unrest.

He heard the voices before he rounded the Whistlestop Diner, while the base of the tower's support structure was still out of view. Not shouting, but containing enough emotion that they carried through the air. Sharp, shrill voices he recognized before he saw the speakers.

"It's too blue, that's all." Betty Hunsaker stood with her arms crossed, neck craned back. "Maybe you're too close to see it when you're up there, but it's perfectly obvious from here."

Sandra, wearing a T-shirt that may once have been white but was now covered in rainbow-smattered stains, maintained a patient smile, though as Jerry drew nearer he thought the corners of her mouth looked a bit strained. "It may look that way now, but when I'm finished I promise you'll be pleased."

"Paint doesn't change color." Frieda shook her head, disapproval carved into the lines on her forehead. "If it's blue now, it'll be blue when you finish."

"Good morning, ladies." Jerry nodded at the three. "What seems to be the problem?"

"Nothing." Betty flashed a sugary smile sideways toward Sandra. "Nothing that can't be corrected, anyway."

The painter caught his gaze in a steady one of her own. "Seems some of the folks in town don't like what they're seeing, so they sent a delegation to tell me about it."

Jerry arched his eyebrows. "That true, Frieda?"

The woman didn't meet his eye. "Well, not an *official* delegation. We just wanted to offer our assistance before it was too late to fix the obvious problems."

He stared upward. Splashes of color on the tower's barrel interrupted the uniform gray in an uneven pattern. "I don't see anything I'd call a problem." He cocked his head. "In fact, I don't see anything at all."

Sandra laughed, a deep, booming sound of mirth worthy of a Texan. "Not much there to see yet, is there?"

Betty's tone became the slightest bit condescending. "Is that blue down at the bottom supposed to be grass?"

"What's that squiggly line running through the grass?" Frieda pulled a piece of paper out of her pocket and opened it. Jerry recognized a copy of Sandra's sketch for her artwork, the one included in the proposal that had won her the painting job. They'd posted it on the town's website along with the minutes from the council meeting.

Frieda traced a line on the paper. "If that's the creek, it's too high. And is that blotch in the sky a goose? Looks more like a woodpecker."

The artist exercised more patience than Jerry could have managed. "I'm testing the colors. You can look at paint in a can all day long, but you don't know what you've got until you see it in use."

That stopped the complaining for a moment while the pair exchanged a glance.

Betty sniffed. "Then I hope it's as obvious to you as it is to the rest of us that the colors you've chosen are all wrong."

"When they're layered they'll look completely different," Sandra explained. "Trust me. I've done this before."

A chilly smile flashed onto Frieda's face. "I'm sure you have. But when you're finished, you'll leave town. Those of us who live here will have to look at these colors for years."

From where he stood, Jerry watched Sandra's jaw bulge slightly as she clenched her teeth. Time to intervene before the woman blew a gasket.

He stepped between Betty and Frieda. "I'm sure Sandra appreciates your feedback, but I think we can leave this to her judgment." Placing an arm behind each of them, he exerted gentle pressure to lead them away. They dug in their heels.

"We were on our way to your office next," Frieda informed him. "Since you're here, you've saved us the trip."

Betty stepped away from his hand and turned on him, her expression stern. "How could you give a business license to that Love woman?"

His mind blanked out for a moment. With a shift of mental gears, he remembered. "Do you mean the massage therapist?"

"If that's what she wants to call herself." Frieda sniffed. "And right on Main Street across from my shop. It's indecent."

For a moment all he could do was blink. "It's a legitimate business. And Ms. Love bought the building."

"It's not an appropriate addition to our town," Betty insisted. "Goose Creek is a wholesome, family-oriented community."

Sandra, eyes round, edged a few inches backward. Out of the line of fire, maybe?

Jerry stood his ground. Obviously these two staunchly upright women had the wrong idea. "I fail to see anything unwholesome about massage therapy. There's nothing more relaxing than a good massage. Works great for tension headaches, too."

Her mouth a disapproving line, Frieda openly leveled a glare on him. "No good will come of it, you mark my words."

She whirled and stomped away. Casting an apologetic but no less determined smile his way, Betty followed.

Speaking of tension headaches, pinpricks of pain stabbed inside Jerry's skull.

"This sure is a small town," Sandra commented when they'd disappeared around the corner of the diner.

"You have no idea." He massaged his temples. "I'm sorry about that. I'll do what I can to keep them at bay, but I can't guarantee you won't have more spectators as the painting progresses."

"Everyone's an art critic." She snorted, and then shrugged. "I was hoping it wouldn't come to this, but I guess I'll have to go undercover." Then she brightened. "Might work out for the best. We can have a big reveal when it's done."

With a promise to help any way he could, Jerry headed back to his office.

❊

Hiding a wince at a stab of pain in her right shoulder, Susan lifted a forty-pound beagle off the metal exam table. Who would have thought that throwing a softball a couple of dozen times would leave her as stiff as if she'd spent the day hefting fifty-pound bags of dog food?

She set the beagle on the floor and gave her an extra rub behind her floppy ears.

"Apply that ointment once a day, and then give her ears a good rub to work it in," she told the dog's owner. "By tomorrow the itching should stop, but keep using the medicine for seven days."

"I will." The woman shoved the tube of ointment in her purse and took the leash. "Thank you, Dr. Susan."

"You're welcome. Call me if she isn't better by tomorrow night." After jotting a note on the diagnosis sheet, she handed it over. "Give this to Millie on the way out."

The beagle disappeared through the swinging door, and Susan limped into her office. Softball and sandals did *not* mix. For tomorrow's practice she'd be more prepared.

Millie appeared in the doorway. "Have time for a walk-in?"

Her first unscheduled appointment since buying the animal clinic. Susan glanced at the daily appointment sheet. The next patient wasn't scheduled for a half-hour, but she would have fit in this appointment regardless.

"Of course. Anybody we know?"

"No, she just moved to town a few days ago."

A new patient. Was that a sign that business was finally picking up? Her mood considerably lighter, Susan rounded the desk. "Let's go meet her."

They entered the reception area to find a woman seated Indian-style on the floor of the *Kuddly Kitties* room, a brightly colored skirt spread out around her and her lap full of kittens. An impressive quantity of blonde curls had been more-or-less contained beneath a red bandana, though rebellious locks escaped to dangle past the tanned shoulders. At their approach, she turned a wide grin upward.

"Look what I found in my building. Aren't they absolutely ambrosial?" She picked up a squirming kitten in a hand with short fingernails painted bright green and held it up to her cheek. "Just so sweet I could eat them all up."

*Ambrosial?* Susan exchanged a glance with Millie, whose smile looked the slightest bit forced.

"Dr. Susan Jeffries, this is Tuesday Love. She's new to Goose Creek."

Since the woman made no effort to stand, Susan bent to shake her hand. "What an interesting name."

"Everybody says so." A girlish giggle escaped her throat. From any other woman well into middle age that would sound odd, but it somehow felt entirely appropriate from this one. "The story behind it is even more interesting."

Millie's eyes went round, and she broke in hastily. "Tuesday is planning to open a business on Main Street."

"Oh?" One of the kittens wobbled on her knee, and Susan bent to scoop the baby up before it tumbled off. "A shop of some sort?"

"Kind of. Not only that, but turns out we're neighbors. I'm renting a house one street over that way." She jerked her head toward the clinic's rear wall and rescued another adventurous climber. "These critters have sharp little claws. I've never had a cat, so I didn't know they had so many toes."

"Most of them don't." Susan examined the one she held. Polydactyl, of course. Most of the cats she'd treated in Goose Creek were. "It's a mu—" At Millie's warning expression, she changed her phrase. "It's a feature we see often here in Goose Creek. Cat owners here are extremely proud of their six-toed pets. The gene was introduced to town five years ago by a tomcat from Key West, Florida."

"How fun." Tuesday picked up another and rubbed noses with it. "How old are they?"

Eyes open, ears newly erect. Susan put her pinkie into the little mouth and felt a row of small but fully developed teeth. "Between three and four weeks, I'd say. You found them?"

Blonde curls waved in the air when Tuesday nodded. "I was cleaning out my building downtown and heard them crying. They were upstairs in a closet." She chucked her finger under a kitten's chin and spoke to it in baby tones. "Your mommy is taking care of you, though. She made you a nest out of a pile of old canvas. I'll bet she'll be upset when she comes back and finds you missing." She looked up. "But I couldn't just leave them there. I'm going to be painting soon, and the fumes might get to them."

Yes, the kittens all looked well-fed.

Millie snapped her fingers. "I think I know where they came from. I heard Kate Farraway say at church last week that her cat had given birth and then hid her kittens somewhere. I'll give her a call."

While Millie returned to the reception desk to look up the number, Susan helped Tuesday gather the six kittens and return them to the towel-lined salad bowl she'd brought them in. She was about to suggest that she perform a quick exam when the door opened and Daddy entered.

"Good morning," he said.

"Morning," she mumbled while avoiding his gaze. Her feelings were still smarting from the lecture she'd endured after softball practice last night.

Tuesday's eyes took on an admiring gleam. "And a good morning to *you*." She somehow made the greeting sound like an invitation. Holding the bowl of kittens in both hands, she rose gracefully from her cross-legged position on the floor, gaze fixed on Daddy.

Daddy's eyes moved as he inspected her from the top-down, ending on the salad bowl. One eyebrow cocked slightly, but instead of voicing a question, he nodded a polite greeting at Tuesday and focused instead on Susan.

"I was hoping we could continue our discussion. Do you have a moment?"

She bit back a quick explanation of the difference between *discussing* and *chastising*.

"We're about finished here." Tuesday stepped close to him. "She was helping me figure out where these babies came from."

Again a look from Daddy, this one containing a touch of a chill. "Then you won't mind if we excuse ourselves and go to Susan's office."

Irritation rubbed across Susan's nerves. How could he treat her customer with anything less than complete courtesy? Or someone who could be a customer, for all he knew.

She stepped forward and took the bowl. "Actually, I am about ready to conduct an examination on these kittens. We'll have to talk later, Daddy."

"This is your father?" Tuesday's gaze bounced between the two of them. "You must take after your mama. I'm sure she's a beauty too?"

Her tone ended in an unmistakable question, and the direct look she fixed on Susan left no doubt as to her query. Susan bit back a grin. Women found Daddy attractive, but he'd never shown the slightest interest in anyone as far back as she could remember. The often-repeated advice he gave his daughter apparently held true to him as well—romantic entanglements were a distraction best avoided.

Wouldn't it be funny if...

"My mother died when I was little." Susan paused, and then acted as though she'd just realized something. "Where are my manners? Ms. Love, this is my father, Thomas Jeffries."

"Call me Tuesday." She cut her eyes sideways and fluttered her eyelashes. "I hope we'll be first-name friends."

A purplish stain colored Daddy's forehead, and Susan rushed to speak before he said something rude. "Tuesday just bought a building here in Goose Creek to open her new business."

"Well, the business isn't new, just the location." She inched closer so that her bare arm nearly touched his. "I've been a massage therapist for more years than I like to claim."

His eyes widened and he stared down the length of his nose at her. "Massage therapist?"

"You bet, honey. The best there is. Why, spend an hour on my table and you'll be so relaxed your legs won't be able to hold you up."

Susan had to struggle not to laugh at the shocked expression on her father's face. Rarely had she seen Daddy rendered speechless.

Tuesday appeared to take the silence for acceptance. "Here. Let me give you a sample."

Before Susan knew what the woman intended, she stepped behind Daddy, placed her hands on both his shoulders, and began kneading. Obviously surprised, Daddy didn't move and his face drained of color.

"Would you feel that?" Tuesday exclaimed. "Shew, honey, your muscles are so tight it's like massaging a wall."

Daddy stepped forward like a horse out of the starting gate, leaving her standing with her hands in the air. "My muscles are fine."

Tuesday came around to face him. "Honey, you need me in the worst way." A smile curved her full lips. "I can help you get rid of some of that stress."

Susan found herself thoroughly enjoying Daddy's discomfort. A little stress reduction was exactly what he needed.

"Susan, I see you're busy. I'll come back later." He edged toward the door, gaze fixed on Tuesday as though ready to make a dash for it if she moved toward him. "Nice to meet you, Ms...." He appeared to choke over her name.

"Just Tuesday, honey." She awarded him an inviting grin. "But as I like to tell my clients, I'm available any day of the week."

He gulped, and the door shut firmly behind him.

Behind the reception desk, Millie's mouth hung open. She fixed Tuesday with a scandalized stare. Between Millie's and Daddy's reactions, Susan fought the urge to laugh. She could not remember ever seeing her father so uncomfortable.

In the next moment, guilt settled over her. Poor Daddy. He really did have a lot of stress, no doubt mostly caused by her.

Tuesday wilted against the door and fanned her face with an exaggerated gesture. "Girl, your daddy is one nice-looking man." Then she hefted herself upright and gestured toward the bowl. "So should I leave those kitties with you, or what?"

Susan looked at Millie, who jerked upright. "Oh. Kate said Bulah's been coming home to eat every morning, but she was afraid to confine her in the house because she knew she was nursing those kittens somewhere. Today Bulah seems fretful, just wandering around the yard. She'll bring her over in an hour or so."

Susan rescued an inquisitive kitty who had climbed on his brothers' backs and was about to launch himself over the side of the bowl. "Sounds like that's our missing mother cat."

Tuesday said to Millie, "Would you tell your friend I'd like to have one if they're not all promised? I couldn't have a pet in my apartment in Indianapolis." Millie nodded, and Tuesday opened the door. Before she disappeared through it, she turned a grin on Susan. "And tell your daddy I hope to see him again. Toodles, girls!"

The last thing Susan saw was a set of green fingernails waving in the air.

# Goose Creek Softball Team

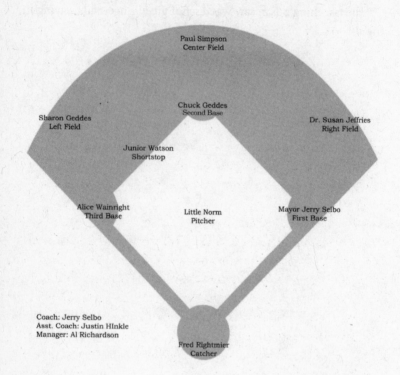

Paul Simpson
Center Field

Chuck Geddes
Second Base

Sharon Geddes
Left Field

Dr. Susan Jeffries
Right Field

Junior Watson
Shortstop

Alice Wainright
Third Base

Little Norm
Pitcher

Mayor Jerry Selbo
First Base

Coach: Jerry Selbo
Asst. Coach: Justin HInkle
Manager: Al Richardson

Fred Rightmier
Catcher

# Chapter Six

The regular contingent of Creekers crowded the soda fountain when Al entered Cardwell's on Saturday morning. A chorus of greetings were called out to him as he scanned the room for an empty chair.

"Over here, Bert. I saved you a seat."

A waving hand caught his eye as Thacker's voice grated on his nerves. Since there was no other option, Al made his way to one of the tables beyond the counter and claimed the vacant seat. Paul and Woody, the other two at the table, were engaged in a conversation with Fred and Jerry at the next table over.

Lucy set a steaming mug in front of Al. He opened his mouth, but before he could voice the request, she pulled the bear-shaped bottle from a deep pocket of her apron and plunked it down.

"You're welcome," she said before he could thank her.

As he stirred honey into his coffee, Thacker made a show of inspecting his wristwatch.

"Slept in today, huh Bert?"

Al set his teeth and continued stirring. He'd learned over the years that responding to Thacker's playful but irritating jabs only encouraged him.

Instead, he glanced around and asked a question of the room at large. "I thought Norman would be here. Anybody heard how he's doing?"

Chuck swiveled on his stool to answer. "He's fine. Planted in his recliner with his foot propped up on pillows, and Little Norm says he's gonna have a sprained finger to match his ankle if he doesn't put down the remote control and give it a rest every now and then."

Jerry turned in his chair. "Hey Al, can you stop by my office before you head home? I want to go over the positions before practice this afternoon."

"I'm free," Thacker answered before Al could do more than open his mouth. "And I've got some 411 you might want to consider."

Jerry turned a polite expression on Thacker. "How's your program coming?"

"Great. I finished it last night and stayed up late running the algorithms. Want to see?" He pulled an oversized cell phone from his breast pocket and tapped on the screen. "I can access the report from here."

Curious in spite of himself, Al waited for Thacker to pull up his report. Across the table, Paul craned his neck to get a better view.

"Okey-dokey, here we are." Thacker turned the phone toward Jerry. "Of course the accuracy will improve when I input more data."

Jerry's forehead wrinkled. "I'm not sure what I'm looking at."

Paul traced a finger in an arc across the screen. "Do those lines represent players?"

"Sort of. They're performance projections. This one right here"— Thacker pointed—"says you need to spiff up your batting average."

Confusion settled on Paul's face. "How do you figure that? I only batted twice Thursday night, and I got two hits."

Thacker threw back his head and laughed. "Not much of an analyst are you, old boy?"

Paul bristled, and Al spared a sympathetic thought for the man. He'd been on the receiving end of Thacker's careless joking often enough.

Thacker went on. "See, both of those pitches were high, but when you were catching, you fumbled whenever the ball approached at a twenty degree angle. The Morleyville pitcher isn't going to take it as easy on you as Little Norm." He turned his attention to Fred. "And you'd better work on those pop-ups, buddy. Don't want to give any runs away, do we? In fact, my data indicates you might do better on third base."

Angry red splotches appeared on Fred's cheeks. "I've been playing catcher since I was a kid in Little League."

"Yeah, that's been a few years and a few pounds ago, huh?" One of Thacker's obnoxious laughs rang in the sudden silence of the drugstore while Fred stiffened.

For a moment Al, who sat between the two, considered edging out of the way. How Thacker could laugh in the face of the half-dozen or so hostile stares was beyond him.

On the other hand, this was Franklin Thacker, Mr. Oblivious.

Ever the diplomat, Jerry's calm voice broke the silence. "I'm sure Fred will do fine as our catcher."

Thacker shrugged, clearly in disagreement. "You're the coach. But you might think about replacing your shortstop. According to my program—"

"I'll tell you what." Jerry rushed to cut him off. "Why don't we go over your report in my office? I'm interested in hearing what you have to say."

"Great. I'll run home and print off a copy." Thacker dug in his pocket for a couple of dollars, which he tossed on the table. "See you in twenty or so?"

Jerry nodded, and Thacker hurried out the door. Al watched through the front window as he paced down the sidewalk with a purposeful stride. When Al turned back to his coffee he found himself the object of several glares.

"He's not my fault," he said defensively.

Paul leaned across the table. "He's your friend."

Al opened his mouth to voice a hot protest, but guilt stilled his tongue. Though he certainly didn't list Thacker among his friends, it was his fault the man had moved to Goose Creek. Rather, Millie was at fault, but a man couldn't throw his wife under the bus, Thacker or not.

Chuck tapped the table with a soda straw. "If he brings those reports to practice tonight and tells my wife what she needs to work on, she'll snap his head off."

"Yeah?" Fred gave a snort. "Junior will do more than that."

The idea of what Junior's ham-sized fists could do to a nerdy guy like Thatcher sent a shudder rippling through Al's frame. And Junior was hot-headed enough to start a fracas without regard for the consequences.

"He's only trying to help."

As soon as the words left his mouth, shock slapped Al backward against his chair. If anyone had told him he would ever utter a word in Franklin Thacker's defense, he would have called them nuts. But he couldn't stand by and let anyone be pummeled, either verbally or physically.

Jerry held up a hand, palm splayed. "Everybody calm down. Al and I will talk to him. Right, Al?"

Slumped in his seat, Al nodded. As the team's manager, it was his job to help the coach, no matter how unpleasant the task. Something else that was all Millie's fault.

❄

Helping, as far as Al was concerned, meant providing a supportive, if silent, presence while Jerry did the talking.

"But I thought they'd want to know." Thacker tapped on the multicolored graph he'd spread out on the mayor's desk. "Data doesn't lie. If they'll pay attention to my analysis, their skills will improve. I guarantee it."

Jerry folded his hands and rested them on the shiny surface

between them. "That may be, but these aren't professional ball players. They're small-town citizens playing a friendly game on the Fourth of July. And they aren't fond of having their weaknesses pointed out."

"Surely you can see it, though." Thacker shoved the paper across the desk. "Your shortstop is too slow. He'd be more successful on first."

"That may be true, but there are other considerations here." The mayor heaved a sigh. "If I don't let him play shortstop, he'll quit."

"It's because I'm new, isn't it?" The chair creaked as Thacker slumped back. "They haven't accepted me yet."

"That may be part of the reason," Jerry agreed. "Goose Creek is a small town in more than geography."

Thacker rounded on Al. "Then you tell them. You're a computer guy like me, but you're a Goose. They'll listen to you."

A thousand excuses shot into Al's brain, but he rejected them all. Sometimes the truth had to be told. He leaned forward, arms resting on his legs, and held Thacker's gaze. "You offended them, Franklin. They aren't going to accept your analysis no matter who presents it."

True confusion erupted on the man's face. "How did I offend them?"

Al had always assumed Thacker was annoying on purpose. Maybe he really wasn't aware of how irritating he could be.

"Diplomacy is not your strong point," Al pointed out.

Instead of reacting defensively, Thacker responded with a slow and thoughtful nod. "That's true. I can see that."

Jerry's voice held a note of apology. "I know you're trying to help, but I think it's best if you don't collect any more data from our practices."

Thacker's lips pursed as he ingested the news he'd just heard. "Okay. I'll leave my tablet at home." Then he slapped his hands on the arms of his chair and rose. "But I'm still going to think of some way to help the team. You wait and see. I'll be a Goose yet."

❋

Thomas emerged from his Lexus in the animal clinic's parking lot and circled Susan's car, inspecting the tires. The front driver's side looked a little low. He made a mental note to check her tire pressure. When she lived at home he'd always kept her car in good running condition, and even when she went to college he made sure the car was inspected by a mechanic one weekend each month.

That was yet another reason moving to Goose Creek was a good idea. Who would watch out for his daughter if he didn't?

A name popped into his head, and he tightened his lips. Hinkle might *think* he could fill the gap left vacant when Susan moved two hundred miles away from her home, but he was mistaken. Thomas had taken care of his daughter her entire life. He wasn't about to hand the responsibility over to a nail-pounding biker with no education.

He entered the clinic to find a satisfying number of clients in the waiting room. The woman behind the desk, Ethel or Hazel or something like that, greeted him with a curt nod before returning to her perusal of the computer monitor. Probably surfing the Internet. Of Susan's three receptionists, he least approved of this Saturday woman. She provided nothing more than a body in the chair as far as he was concerned. The new afternoon girl, Alice, was little better. A mouse of a woman who rarely spoke above a whisper, though at least she paid attention to the clients. If only the regular receptionist, Millie, would stay on full time. A competent woman, she really ran the desk.

Her only major flaw was her approval of Hinkle. A competent receptionist, but obviously lacking in character judgment.

The clinic door swung open and Susan appeared, followed by a yellow dog—a mongrel, by the looks of it—with a child holding the end of the leash. The boy's mother clutched several sample packets of dog food.

"Try that sweet potato formula," Susan was saying, "and let me know if you see an improvement in the scratching."

"Gluten intolerant." The woman clucked her tongue. "Who would have thought?"

Susan caught sight of him. "Hi, Daddy. You're bright and early this morning."

The sight of her smile settled a tense knot in his stomach. They'd been at odds so often lately that that smile didn't appear nearly as much as it used to.

*Thanks to Hinkle.*

Using care, he replied in a pleasant tone. "I thought I'd check the books while you worked, and then we can review them together over dinner this evening."

The smile faltered. She switched her attention to the boy, who waved farewell as he led his dog outside. Then she caught the eye of a woman in the waiting area holding a Chihuahua. "I'll be right with you, Mrs. Baker." She looked back in his direction but did not meet his gaze. "Daddy, could I speak with you privately?"

"Of course."

He followed her around the desk as the receptionist slid the last customer's check into the cashbox and returned to her inspection of the computer monitor. A glance as he passed confirmed his suspicion. Facebook. Susan would have to speak with her about that.

At the end of the short hallway Susan stopped. "Daddy, I have softball practice at five o'clock, and then Justin and I are going out. I told you yesterday."

With an effort, he managed not to scowl at the mention of Hinkle's name. "And I told you that you need to stay on top of your accounting."

"Yes, of course, but it doesn't have to be tonight."

"Saturday is the logical time to close out the work week." He allowed a note of chiding to enter his voice. "We've discussed this before, Susan."

"I know we have." She smoothed a lock of hair behind her ear, a gesture she'd picked up as a child that appeared whenever she was uncomfortable. "But this softball thing is only for a month, and then I can return to a normal schedule."

She might say that, but Thomas knew better. That ridiculous ballgame was Hinkle's maneuver to monopolize her time. When the game ended, he'd finagle something else to entice her away from her priorities.

He folded his arms across his chest and fixed her with a stern look. "May I remind you that I have invested a significant amount of money in your business? I can't afford to lose my investment while you play games."

Her head shot up and her eyes locked onto his. They gleamed with something that Thomas was not accustomed to seeing in his daughter—defiance. The rigid set of her jaw left a distinctly uncomfortable feeling in the pit of his stomach.

"I'm well aware of your investment and my obligation to you. You remind me often enough."

When had this rebellious streak appeared in his passive, obedient daughter? With Hinkle, of course. Since he rumbled into town on that motorcycle, Thomas's relationship with Susan had become increasingly strained.

"This is not the place to have this discussion." He gestured toward the waiting room. "You have clients waiting. I'll check the books while you work, and we can go over them together." He ground out the last, though the effort cost him. "Whenever you have time."

For a moment she didn't reply. Then she inclined her head. "You can use my office."

When she headed for the reception area, Thomas entered the office to find a large, flat box leaning against the nearest wall.

"What's this?"

She spoke over her shoulder. "The box? It's a gate for the dog run out back. The old one is rickety and won't stay closed. Justin's going to install it this afternoon before softball practice."

Hinkle again. Thomas scowled, but Susan had already disappeared through the swinging door so he turned his glare on the box. There was a time when she relied on him for anything that needed to be repaired. Why was this the first mention he'd heard of replacing the gate? He'd been in town for a full week already, willing to do whatever it took to make their joint venture a success, and so far he'd done nothing except deskwork. True, that was his forte, but he was perfectly capable of minor repairs as well. It didn't take a genius to wield a wrench.

First he'd take a look at the existing gate and then gather the necessary tools. When he opened the back door, warm, humid air rushed into the room. The temperature must be nearly eighty already and noon was still hours away. Yet another reason to get the gate hung now, before the full heat of the day.

He inspected the gate. Definitely ready for the garbage heap. One hinge was so loose the whole thing sat cockeyed. A broken latch dangled from the top and the side bar was bent like someone had pried it with a crowbar. Two concrete blocks, one on either side, were the only things holding the gate closed. He cast a glance back toward the clinic. Susan should have ensured that the previous owner replaced this gate before she bought the business. If he'd been here, he would have done so. Even more proof that his moving to Goose Creek was a good idea.

"Helloooo!" A female voice carried to him through the heavy air.

The clinic backed up to an empty lot on a residential street. On either side of the lot sat a row of older homes, small wooden structures built decades ago. Most were not in the best state of repair. Paint peeled on the lopsided back porch of the house directly catty-corner to the clinic's fence.

"Over here, Thomas."

When he located the caller, a groan escaped his throat. What was that Tuesday woman doing here?

She stood at the corner of a yard two houses down the row, waving enthusiastically in his direction. The waist-high wooden fence enclosing her yard leaned at an alarming angle against a row of scraggly bushes.

He raised a tentative hand to return her wave and immediately regretted the action. Apparently she took the gesture as an invitation. She opened a rickety gate in far greater need of repair than the one he was about to replace and hurried through the unmown grass on bare feet. A muddy garden trowel dangled from one hand.

"There I was, digging up an old dead bush, and when I looked up there you were." She fixed a wide smile on him. "I was hoping to see you again but didn't dream it would be so soon."

"Yes, well." He cleared his throat and dropped his gaze from the eager sparkle in her eyes. "I'm helping my daughter with a few tasks."

"Ah." When she nodded, her hair floated around her head like Medusa's snakes. "She's lucky to have a helpful papa like you."

At least the woman possessed a shred of insight.

"She's accustomed to depending on me, since we only have each other."

"Yeah, she told me about you losing your wife." She brushed at a stray curl with the back of a dirt-encrusted hand. "That had to be hard, raising a little girl on your own."

"We managed." Discussions of this sort, especially with strangers, left him uneasy. He bent to grasp the first concrete block and move it out of the way. Maybe if he started working she would take the hint.

"Bend those knees, Thomas." She pointed with her trowel. "You'll hurt your back otherwise."

The last thing he needed was advice from a woman with dirty green fingernails. Straightening, he gave her a glance down the length of his nose. "Don't let me keep you from your bush."

"Hmm." Sparkling eyes narrowed in a knowing look, and then her lips twisted into a sideways grin. "Okay. But if you run out of things to do, I've got plenty. Toodles!"

He watched her retreat, stepping high through calf-length grass, her hair waving like a willow tree in the wind. Bending once again to his task, he grasped the edges of the concrete block and tugged. Heavier than expected, the thing didn't budge. One side had sunk into the dirt and become wedged. Rearranging his hands, he gathered his strength and pulled.

"Umph!"

Pain shot through his lower back, sharp enough to bring tears to his eyes.

Drat the woman, she had cursed him.

He released the block and tried to straighten, a fist pressed against his spine. The muscle went into a spasm that felt like a spear being shoved through his back. A cry flew unbidden from his mouth and he wavered.

"Thomas! Oh no!"

Leaning heavily on the gate's support post, he fought the sting of tears. Tuesday's feet appeared in his line of vision.

"Are you all right?"

*No,* he wanted to shout. *Someone is stabbing my back with a hot poker.* "Fine," he managed to grind out.

"No you're not. I told you to bend your knees, didn't I?"

Never had he wanted so badly to tell a woman to shut up, but at the moment he had no breath to spare.

She grabbed the outside concrete block in her grubby hands and—knees bent—rolled it out of the way. The gate swung outward and she rushed to his side.

"Tell me where it hurts." Surprisingly gentle fingers moved his fist and prodded his back.

"Ow! Don't touch me." He tried to twist away, and the movement increased his agony so that he nearly collapsed.

"Come on, let's get you inside."

"No," he said quickly. If Susan saw him like this she'd think he was getting old and useless. He straightened slowly, his jaw set against the pain. "I'll be okay. Just give me a minute."

"Hmm." Tuesday planted her hands on her hips and tilted her head. Once again, insight sparked in her eyes, leaving Thomas with the uncomfortable feeling that she knew exactly why he didn't want to be led inside the clinic like an invalid. "If you ignore that muscle, it's going to tighten up on you. By tomorrow you won't be able to walk. If you can walk now, that is."

"I'll take aspirin or something."

She blew a raspberry through pursed lips. "You want to burn a hole in your stomach lining on top of everything else? Come on." She stepped close and tried to slip her arm around him.

Jerking away resulted in more pain, but at least she halted. "What are you doing?"

"I'm taking you to my house. What you need is a massage and some ice."

When he would have protested, she crossed her arms and pierced him with an unyielding stare. "If you don't, I'm going to march inside right now and get your little girl to come talk sense into you."

Cornered, that's what he was. He could go around the building and attempt to limp to his car and hope the receptionist was so wrapped up in Facebook that she didn't notice him through the window. Or that none of the customers in the waiting room saw him. Or Susan herself.

Pouring all the dignity he could muster into his voice, he said, "It seems I have no choice."

"A good decision. Trust me, I know what I'm doing."

He allowed her to take his arm and lead him slowly across the uneven ground, feeling like a hobbled prisoner being led to the firing squad.

❈

Boxes crowded the small living room, some stacked three high. One cushion on a worn sofa was clear, and a stack of books covered the seat of an armchair.

"You just moved to town?" Thomas asked. Not that he cared particularly, but at the moment he was under attack by a fit of nerves.

What would people think if they found him with Tuesday Love alone in her house?

"A couple of days ago." Tuesday bent to shove a box out of the way and started down a short hallway. "Come on back to the bedroom."

He halted. Under no circumstances would he enter her bedroom.

Turning, she peered at him and broke into laughter. "The look on your face. Are you afraid I'll try to seduce you or something?"

No safe answer came to mind, so he remained silent and looked anywhere but at her.

"My massage table is set up in there. I sleep upstairs." She ducked her head to catch his eye and spoke as if coaxing a child into the dentist's chair. "Come on, Thomas. You're perfectly safe."

"I'm not afraid," he said quickly. The moment the words left his mouth he realized how childish they sounded.

"Of course not, not a big strong man like you." She smiled encouragement down the hallway.

His back throbbed, and he fought to hide a wince. Since he'd come this far, he might as well go through with it.

Like the living room, this room was tiny. No boxes here, though. Instead, a narrow cushioned table stood in the exact center. A rolling stool such as a doctor might use had been pushed into one corner, and a small desk rested against the back wall.

"You're in luck." Tuesday crossed to a table in the corner and switched on a miniature waterfall. "My table is the first thing I set up. I want to be ready for potential clients even before I open my business." Beside the waterfall sat a compact stereo, which she also turned on. Soft music began to play.

She pulled down a window shade to darken the room, and then faced him. "I'm going to step out in the hall while you take your clothes off."

"What?" He jerked upright, an unwise movement that sent pain shafting across his back. What kind of place was she running? "No. Absolutely not."

Hands planted on her hips, she twisted her lips. "How do you expect me to work your muscles with your clothes on?"

"It's my back that's hurt, not the rest of me." He put on his most obstinate expression.

"Fine." She waved a hand in the air. "Leave your pants on, but the shirt comes off. Lie face-down on the table and cover up with that sheet. Let me know when you're ready."

Alone in the room, Thomas stood where he was and considered his options. Should he leave now and put an end to this awkward situation? The sharp pain in his back indicated some sort of damage, probably a tweaked muscle. If he were back home in Paducah he would phone his doctor. Here, he'd be forced to choose someone out of the phone book or go to a walk-in clinic. Certainly there were none of those here in Goose Creek, which meant he'd have to make the forty-minute drive to Lexington. At the idea of sitting in a car for even a few minutes, the pain intensified.

Since he was already here...

Moving cautiously, he unbuttoned and removed his shirt and then climbed up on the table. The faint odor of honeysuckle filled the air when he unfolded the sheet and awkwardly draped it over his body. A round cushion with a hole in the center provided support for his head while allowing him to breathe. When he achieved a prone position, the muscles all over his back convulsed as they adjusted to the new arrangement. He lay still, breath caught in his lungs, and waited for the pain to subside.

"Are you ready?" Tuesday's voice came from the other side of the door.

"I suppose."

The door opened and closed, though his range of vision was limited to a two-foot radius directly beneath his face. Her feet—still bare and bearing signs of her yard work—appeared. A hand touched the middle of his back, warm and gentle.

"Relax, Thomas. You're so tight I'm surprised you can move at all."

Her fingers slid across his back to his shoulder blade and began to rub in a circular motion.

"The pain is lower."

"I know, but first I'm going to work the surrounding area. Working the sore place won't do any good if the rest of your back is rigid. It'll only put pressure on the injured muscle." She tapped his shoulder. "Really, try to relax. You're all tensed up."

His shoulders *were* tense. Until she mentioned it, he hadn't realized how stiffly he held himself. With an effort, he forced his muscles to loosen.

"That's better. Ooh, here's a bad one." The pressure increased, and a muscle inside his shoulder blade jumped as her fingers pushed across it. "You must have a really stressful job. What do you do?"

"I'm the vice president of investments at a bank in Paducah."

"I figured it was something important like that. You don't get muscles this tight flipping burgers." She changed positions and her hands found another knot, which she began to massage.

Though there were stresses aplenty at the bank, his biggest cause for tension lately was a motorcycle-riding handyman with designs on his daughter. But he wasn't about to discuss his private business.

She fell silent, which suited him fine. This situation was awkward enough without the burden of conversing with someone with whom he had nothing in common. He closed his eyes, listening to the combination of soft music and the gentle trickle of water. Remarkably relaxing, actually. Maybe he should consider getting a water feature for his house when he moved here.

Interesting how his muscles truly did relax as she massaged them. Already his shoulders felt less tense, and the pain in his lower back had diminished. That might be attributed to lying prone and not moving, but without a doubt Tuesday was a skilled masseuse. Not that he had any prior experiences with which to compare.

As her ministrations crept lower on his back, he set his teeth in anticipation of the moment when she would reach the painful area.

Her touch became feather-soft as she probed. Within seconds she honed in on the injured muscle.

"Is this the place?"

"Yes. Be careful, please."

She kneaded with increasing pressure, and though definitely painful, her actions were surprisingly gentle. And effective. He almost felt the rigid muscle unlock and could not suppress a soft, "Ahhh."

"Feels good, huh?"

"Not good." He wasn't ready to go that far. "But beneficial."

"Told you so." Her giggle blended with the relaxing music, not nearly as irritating as before.

Several comebacks came to mind, but he held his tongue and continued to enjoy the relaxing effect of the massage.

By the time she finished with his back, the stabbing pain had been reduced to a dull ache. She removed her hands, and a surprising wave of regret flooded him. Was his massage over already? He felt the sheet being lifted from his feet.

"Thomas! You're still wearing your shoes," she scolded.

"My feet are fine." He lifted his head from the cushioned headrest, preparatory to climbing off the table.

"You may think so, but I studied reflexology in massage school. Certain areas of your feet are linked to other parts of your body. A foot massage can release endorphins that help with pain."

She tugged his shoe off. Normally he would have resisted, but just then he felt so relaxed he wasn't eager to end the massage. His sock was peeled off as well.

"Would you look at that?"

"What?" He lifted his head and craned his neck to look over his shoulder.

"I thought you held all your stress in your shoulders, but I was wrong." She giggled again. "Your toes are curled up tighter than a scared roly-poly bug."

Indignant, he said, "They are not," as he willed his toes to unclench.

"Yeah? Lookie here." She came around to the head of the table and thrust a sock into view. She'd inserted her hand, and pink skin showed through a worn place in the tip. "I'll bet you go through a lot of socks."

He would have argued, but the truth was he did have a tendency to wear holes in his socks, a fact that he had never actively realized and found somehow embarrassing.

"Don't worry." His other shoe and sock were removed. "Just lie back and let me do my work." She sat on the stool, rolled it to the end of the table, and grasped one foot with a firm grip.

At first the endorphin story sounded to Thomas like zen-ified mumbo-jumbo, something for which he had zero patience. But after a few moments he decided there may have been something to the theory. Such an intense relaxation seized him while Tuesday worked on his feet that he found himself dozing off. Even his back stopped throbbing for the duration of the massage.

When she finished, she helped him sit up and placed his shoes and socks beside him, then stood back as he put them on. "You need to drink plenty of water today to flush all the toxins I've worked out of your muscles. And put ice on that back. Twenty minutes on, twenty minutes off."

"Yes, doctor." The good-natured response surprised him even as he uttered it. His mood was much lighter. Endorphins, perhaps? He looked her directly in the eye and poured sincerity into his voice. "Thank you. I feel much better."

"You won't be thanking me tomorrow. The way I worked you over, you're gonna feel like somebody walloped you."

"How much do I owe you?" He pulled his wallet out of his back pocket.

"Not a cent. The first time's on the house." She grinned and fluttered her eyelashes. "Actually, my door's open any time you want to come back."

At the blatantly flirtatious gesture, his previous discomfort returned. Though the woman obviously possessed a measure of skill in her chosen profession, he had no desire to encourage her personal attentions.

"I'll keep that in mind." Contrary to the words, his tone left no doubt that he would not return. He slid his wallet back into his pocket. "Now if you'll excuse me, I need to get back to the animal clinic."

One thing was certain. He would not pursue his idea of putting up the new gate. Leave the manual labor to Hinkle, who was accustomed to toiling and sweating in the hot sun.

# Chapter Seven

Susan leaned against the fence and watched the sun glisten on the exposed strip of skin on the back of Justin's neck while he worked.

"He was acting really odd."

Using both hands, he cranked a wrench and the rusty bolt turned with a screech. "In what way?"

"I don't know." She hooked a finger through the chain link and searched for words to describe Daddy's behavior. "When he first got here, he was obstinate. Insisted that I cancel our plans tonight and go over the clinic's weekly financial activity."

"Well, there you go." The last bolt removed, he grasped the gate with hands encased in thick work gloves and lifted it out of the frame. "You broke the cardinal rule. You chose me over him."

Though he turned one of his charming grins on her, the truth of the words still stung. Why couldn't the two most important people in her life get along?

"Does there have to be a choice?" A pout crept into her voice. "Surely he doesn't expect me to spend every minute with him for the rest of my life."

He carried the crooked gate a few steps away and tossed it in the grass. "That's exactly what he expects. He's quitting his job and moving here to make sure you do." Extracting a razor knife from his tool belt, he knelt on the grass and sliced into the box to free the replacement.

"You make him sound like a tyrant or something."

"Not at all. He's a father who's having a hard time of letting go, that's all. And you're having a hard time pulling away."

The words, though undoubtedly innocently spoken, fell on Susan like blows. "Is that what you think? That I'm overly dependent?"

Justin's face jerked toward her, and his expression softened. He rose, tossed the box cutter on the ground, and came to where she stood. Taking her gently by the shoulders, he pulled her into a hug. "That's not what I meant. I think your relationship with your dad is beautiful. I wish my father had been less dedicated to his job and more committed to me and my kid brother."

Inhaling the combination of scents that were uniquely Justin's—grass, the earthy aroma of rich soil, the lingering hint of soap, even a musky touch of sweat—Susan allowed herself to release some of the pent-up emotion that had grown all afternoon since Daddy disappeared from the clinic. "I must have really upset him. He left without even saying goodbye."

"Suz, listen to me." Justin pulled back to look her in the eye. "Sooner or later we're going to have to face a hard truth. Your father doesn't like me."

"When he gets to know you he will."

He shook his head. "I've tried, and I'll keep on trying, but the fact is he thinks I'm not good enough for his little girl." A dimple carved the tanned skin beside his mouth, and her stomach flip-flopped. "Actually, he's right about that."

"Don't be silly."

"He may never thaw enough to like me. If we keep going with this relationship, he'll blame me for taking his daughter away from him. He'll probably end up hating me."

Though she would like to disagree, a dismal truth rang in his words. A lump formed in her throat around which her breath felt ragged.

"My biggest fear," he whispered, holding her eyes in a gaze that let her peek into his soul, "is that his disapproval will end up damaging your feelings for me down the road."

Fighting tears, she shook her head. "That won't happen."

He placed a finger on her lips. "Never say never, Suz. He's your dad. You need to decide if you can handle living with a conflict that may never end."

Leaning forward, he placed a soft kiss on her forehead and then returned to his work.

Any answer she might have made lodged behind the lump in her throat.

❋

Jerry pitched his voice to carry across the pasture where the softball players milled, waiting for the second practice to begin. "All right, everyone gather around home plate."

The number of onlookers had increased. At least two dozen folding chairs lined the fencerow, several blankets spread out picnic-style between them. That could mean the townsfolk had decided to rally around the team, or it might be that word of their incompetency had spread and everyone wanted a good laugh on a Saturday evening. Chiding himself for the dire thought, Jerry forced a pleasant expression as his team assembled.

Little Norm stomped on the scuffed-up polyurethane square. "Where'd we get real bases and stuff?"

"Justin borrowed them from the high school over in Frankfort." Jerry nodded his thanks at Justin.

"Better'n chalk," observed Junior. "We're startin' to look like a real ball team."

While he wouldn't go that far, Jerry didn't correct the man. He glanced around for Al. "Do you have my chart?"

Holding a shiny metal clipboard with the price sticker still stuck to the back, Al retrieved the chart from a thin stack of papers and handed it over. The team gathered behind Jerry to see.

"I've worked up our positions. In left field we'll have Sharon, Paul will take center, and Dr. Susan will cover right field."

The veterinarian looked faintly sick, but when Justin awarded her an encouraging smile, she managed a nod.

"In the infield we'll have Little Norm on the pitcher's mound and Fred as catcher. Junior will play shortstop, as agreed."

The man stuck his thumbs beneath the straps of his overalls and puffed his bare chest.

"Alice will cover third and Chuck second. And I'll be on first, at least until I can recruit someone else." He folded the chart and handed it back to Al, who secured it on his clipboard. "If you know someone who wants to play, encourage them to join us."

He scanned the spectators, ready to call out anyone who looked the slightest bit competent. At the end of the line nearest home plate, Franklin Thacker reclined in a lawn chair making notes on a pad of paper. Catching Jerry's glance, he waved a pen in the air. Apparently their talk this morning hadn't been completely successful. Well, at least he wasn't tapping on his tablet. If he stayed on the sidelines and kept his mouth shut, maybe nobody would notice.

He turned back to his team. "Okay, everyone take your positions. Justin is going to hit some balls for us."

They dispersed. Jerry fought a wave of irritation at Junior's sauntering gait toward the baseline between second and third. A puff of dust kicked up when he turned on his boot heel and planted his feet.

Wait. *Boot heel?*

Yes, the Goose Creek shortstop had chosen to wear heavy work boots to practice. Biting back a groan, Jerry made a mental note to discuss proper footwear before he dismissed the team this evening.

Al set a bucket of softballs near home plate, and Justin stepped into the batter's box. "First we're going to practice fielding the ball just as we'd do in a real game. I'm the batter. Everyone ready?"

"No! Wait!"

The shout came from behind Jerry. He turned to see the veterinarian running toward the infield.

"I forgot to get a glove," she said as she ran past him.

Another groan arose in his throat, which he did not suppress since no one could hear him. Justin helped her select a glove from the plastic tote and awarded her an encouraging smile.

When she had returned to right field, she waved and shouted, "I'm ready."

On the other side of the fence, Jerry's wife had selected a place near first base from which to watch the practice. As he turned, he caught her eye. With a crowd of his constituents watching he didn't dare scowl or do anything else to reflect his gloomy attitude, but Cindie knew him well. She folded her hands as if in prayer and then gave an encouraging thumbs-up.

"All right," Justin shouted. "Get ready. Here comes the first batter."

He began with a line drive straight to Little Norm, who caught it with no problem. The next ball went to Alice, who snagged it out of the air. Jerry caught the next and made a show of stomping on the base. The next went over Chuck's head and though he backed up, the ball bounced a few yards behind him. Paul ran forward from centerfield to scoop it up and cocked his arm back to throw it to second. But second base stood empty. Where was their shortstop? Junior stood on the baseline, feet planted as if rooted in place. Did Junior even know what a shortstop was supposed to do? Instead Paul lobbed it to Chuck, who whirled and made a show of tagging an invisible runner.

"Good fieldwork," Justin called. "Uh, Junior? Next time Chuck has to leave his base, you run over there and cover second for him, okay?"

The man pounded a fist into his glove and nodded. "Sure thing." He turned toward Chuck. "Gotcha covered, buddy."

"Okay, let's try some long ones." Justin lifted his head and projected his voice. "Get ready, Suz. This one's coming to you."

The bat hit the softball with a solid whack. Impressed with Justin's aim, Jerry watched the ball arc through the air above him and descend toward Dr. Susan's position. Raising her glove in the air, a look of sheer panic erupted on the girl's face. As the ball dropped toward her, she hunched down and planted her glove on her head like a hat. The ball bounced two feet to her right. The onlookers released a collective sigh.

"It's okay," Justin shouted. "We'll work on that."

Jerry sought his wife's gaze, but she had her eyes scrunched shut in a wince. The beginnings of a headache twinged, and he pinched the skin between his eyebrows to relieve the pressure. Only seven practices left before the game.

# Chapter Eight

"Do you have a minute, Mrs. Richardson?"

Millie tore her attention from the men destroying her beautiful parlor to look at Justin. He'd come through the back door and stood in the magnificent entry hall, dark hair full of sawdust. At the sight of his cautious expression and tight fists, a frightful uneasiness overtook her. What now?

"Of course. I'm not doing anything helpful here." She cringed as one of the demolition crew hefted a sledgehammer and struck through the wall. He could exhibit a little less enthusiasm, as far as she was concerned. "I hope there's nothing wrong."

"Well..." The young man scrunched his features. "It's not the best news. But it's not as bad as mold in the walls."

She gave a humorless laugh. "I'm not sure many things are. What is it?"

"It's easiest to show you. Come on up to the attic."

The attic? Her mood dipped even lower as she followed Justin up the ornate staircase, down the hallway, and up a second set of stairs, these ones cramped and steep. Rufus trailed along, though he lagged behind as he hefted himself up the stairs. Justin opened the door at the top and Millie stepped into an oppressive heat. A line of sunlight from beneath the deep eaves on all sides did little to alleviate the heavy gloom in the space that ran the length of the house. Thick sheets of insulation that were once probably as pink as her Volkswagen were now gray and dust-covered. She followed him through a layer of dirt to the far end, stepping around the brick column of a chimney. A severe tickle began in her nose as the dust they kicked up rose in a fine cloud, and she sneezed. Goodness, this place needed a good cleaning. But the attic was way down toward the bottom of her list. At the rate the repairs were going, she might get to it in a few years.

"I noticed some damage to the external wood when the guys and I were working on the roof," Justin said as he led her to the back end of the space. "Not surprising, really. The wooden exterior on a house this old doesn't hold up well against years of weather, wind, and sun exposure. But I was pretty sure those holes weren't caused by normal wear and tear."

"Holes?"

"Not huge, but big enough that they need to be repaired. Here, look."

They'd arrived at the end of the attic. Pulling on a pair of work gloves, he squatted down on his haunches and tugged a blanket of insulation away from the wall. Sunlight showed through a hole about a foot long and several inches high. "Oh my. What in the world caused that? Storm damage, maybe?"

She couldn't stop a hopeful tone from creeping into her voice. Her conversation with the insurance agent had revealed the depressing news that mold was considered "hidden and concealed," which was not covered by their policy. Had the damage been as a result of an accident or natural disaster, the repair work would have been covered. No matter how convincingly Millie argued that there could be no bigger disaster, the man refused to budge.

If this hole had been caused by a storm, perhaps the repairs would be paid for.

But Justin shook his head. "No, ma'am. See how those edges are gnawed? This is the work of squirrels."

"Squirrels? Are you sure?"

"'Fraid so. Look here." He planted a boot on the insulation so he could reach a few feet beneath the sloping eaves and pulled back the fluffy stuff to reveal a wad of sticks, leaves, and gray fiberglass. "I found several other nests too, and a lot of damaged wood. A few more holes, but none as big as this one."

"Is the house unsafe?"

"Not at all."

She took comfort from his confidence, but then he continued in a regretful tone.

"But I wouldn't recommend ignoring the problem or they'll continue to cause damage. At the very least we'll need to patch up all the holes and cover the vents with wire mesh. We also need to replace the chimney caps. They're rusted out."

Millie turned and eyed the closest column of bricks. "It looks sturdy from here."

"Oh, it is," he assured her. "A squirrel would be hard-put to chew through brick and mortar. But I found nests in two of the chimneys. Come winter when you want to build a fire, you'll have a big problem on your hands."

With a sigh, she nodded. "I understand." Millie cast a glance toward Rufus, who had refused to enter the attic but watched them from the doorway. They'd never had squirrels at their house on Mulberry Avenue. But the poor dog had been defeated by the bold squirrel population of this house. Or perhaps he was overwhelmed by the sheer number of the fuzzy-tailed rodents.

"Well, do whatever you need to do. I'll call Albert and let him know."

A task she did not relish. Her husband, who had become increasingly dour every day since they moved into this house, would be furious.

※

He was.

"Squirrels in the attic?"

Albert's shout resounded through the phone. Seated alone at the kitchen table, Millie pulled the receiver away from her ear and listened from a distance as he raged.

"I told you this would happen, Millie. Dollar by dollar, dime by dime, that house is bleeding us dry. It's like a giant, hulking vampire, sucking our blood. Not only money, but the never-ending list of chores is exhausting. I work all day and then I come home and work all night too. I'm telling you, we'll end up a couple of empty shells, exhausted and broke."

Normally she would have cajoled him out of his anger, but just then she didn't have the energy. "Don't be dramatic, Albert."

"If there was ever a time for drama, it's now. Those squirrels are ruining my life. They empty the birdfeeders as fast as I can fill them and swarm all over the property. It's not enough that our yard is overrun by squirrels. Now they're infesting our house too? And what about that dog of yours? Why isn't he keeping them under control?"

Millie looked at Rufus, who lay sleeping on his cushion in the corner. "I'm a little worried about him. Do you suppose he's depressed about something?"

"He's a *dog*."

"Dogs can get depressed," she told him. "I read it in a magazine at the clinic. Maybe I'll ask Susan. She might have a medication to recommend."

The spluttering on the other end of the phone continued for some minutes before coherent words formed. When Albert continued, he'd managed to achieve a semblance of control. She had to put the phone up to her ear in order to hear him.

"I want you to call the inspector as soon as we hang up. Ask him why he missed that damage. Tell him we expect him to cover the cost of the repairs."

"Now you're just being silly." She did not bother to filter her annoyance. "Justin said the hole was obscured by the ornamental trim on the outside and by insulation on the inside. If he hadn't seen it when he was crawling all over the roof, he wouldn't have caught it either."

She might as well not have spoken.

"We'll sue the inspector, that's what we'll do."

A crash from the front parlor jerked Millie upright. Now what?

"Can we talk about this when you get home? I need to run. Love you. Bye."

Tossing the phone onto the table, she dashed toward the parlor with Rufus at her heels. When she rounded the corner she found the two workmen standing in a sea of broken glass, their expressions remorseful. A large mirror, which they'd removed from the wall before they started, lay in shards at their feet. Jagged fragments still clung to the inside edges of the gilded frame like razor-sharp teeth, reminiscent of Albert's imaginary vampires.

The shorter man ducked his head in her direction without meeting her eye. "I'm right sorry 'bout that, ma'am. I guess I wasn't paying close enough attention to where I tossed my hammer."

A dozen replies pinged in her head. A sharp reprimand about taking care seemed entirely appropriate. But rebuking strangers went against her nature. She was more inclined to dismiss the incident and tell the poor man not to worry.

Did this constitute an accident? Of course their deductible was so high it wouldn't be worth filing an insurance claim, even though the mirror would probably cost several hundred dollars to replace. Mold Man's advertisement boasted that he was bonded and insured, so perhaps he would cover the cost of the replacement. If he balked, she could threaten a lawsuit.

The thought brought her up short. Goodness, what was becoming of her? Albert's cynicism was rubbing off on her. Richardsons were not people who sued.

She arranged a smile on her face. "Accidents happen. I wasn't crazy about that mirror anyway. Please don't give it another thought."

His tense posture relaxed. "That's real nice of you, ma'am. Thank you."

Oddly, some of her tension dissipated at his obvious relief. What good would it do to rant and rave like Albert? None, and it would raise her blood pressure besides. If she obsessed about every little thing that happened with this house, she'd end up a raving maniac or depressed like Rufus.

"I'll get the broom and dust bin," she told them, and left the room.

❈

Thomas parked his car on the street in front of Tuesday Love's house. For a moment after he turned off the key, he didn't move. If anyone spotted his car here he'd be mortified. But who would see at two in the afternoon? Susan was at work the next street over. The only other person in town who might recognize his Lexus was Hinkle, and he was working at the Richardsons' three miles away.

He sat with his hands on the steering wheel and peered at the house. The roof of a tiny covered porch sagged at one end, held in place by a square beam with a vertical crack near the top. White paint peeled on the siding and porch railing. The black shutters on either side of the front door were in desperate need of attention, large sections of paint chipped away to reveal areas of exposed wood. Yet frilly curtains showed in the windows, and a pair of rosebushes bloomed with furious glory on either side of the porch steps.

What was he doing here? The question had revolved in his mind like a merry-go-round during the drive from Lexington. Saturday's massage, necessitated by his injury, had been spur-of-the-moment. When he bid Tuesday farewell he had expected that would be the last time he stepped foot in her house. That night, sitting in the armchair in his hotel room with a bag of ice at his back, he'd acknowledged the accuracy of the woman's advice. Lots of water and repeating sessions with ice did alleviate some of the pain. That the massage had helped to loosen the twisted muscle he had no doubt. But neither had he any intention of returning.

And yet, here he was.

Part of the reason was the unbelievably restful sleep he'd enjoyed Saturday night. He couldn't remember ever sleeping so well. And though Sunday morning her prediction of sore muscles was proven true, he dreaded the gradual return of tension in his shoulders. And his feet. Now that he'd been made aware of his tendency to clench his toes, relaxing them had become a near obsession. At that very moment they were drawn up tighter than a prize fighter's fists. With an effort, he forced them to straighten as far as they could within the confines of his shoes.

The front door on the house opened. Tuesday emerged wearing a pair of shorts and a tank top, her hair piled on her head. She ducked down to peer through the car window, and Thomas fought the urge to slink down in the seat.

Cupping her hands around her mouth, she shouted, "Is that you, Thomas?"

Drat the woman. Why not paint a sign and hang it on the front door? *Thomas Jeffries is here.*

Since he'd been spotted there was no dignified way to back out. Resigned to going through with his impulsive decision, he exited the car.

"Figured it must be you." Her smile broadened. "I don't know anybody else who drives a fancy car like that."

He hurried down the cracked and uneven sidewalk, glancing right and left to see if they were being observed. Relieved when he saw no one, he mounted the porch steps. "I'm taking my daughter to dinner tonight, and I'm early. But if you're busy, I'll understand."

"I'm never too busy for my favorite client." She hooked her arm through his and pulled him into the house.

The front room held fewer boxes, and she'd hung pictures on the wall. A half-dozen photographs in inexpensive black frames had been arranged on the wall facing the sofa. While she shut the door he examined them. Outdoor scenes depicting fields of wildflowers, a flock of geese floating on a pond, a barn with sunlight slanting through the uneven slats. His attention drawn to a photo of a covered bridge, he admired the artistic angle the photographer had chosen.

"That's quite lovely," he commented.

She stood beside him, her head tilted as she inspected the photo. "Isn't it? One of my sisters has a real knack for taking pictures."

He glanced at her. "One of your sisters? How many do you have?"

"Seven for sure, but probably more. New ones crop up every now and then. Nobody's really sure who Daisy's daddy was, but we claim her anyway."

Though he knew it was rude, he couldn't stop his jaw from dangling.

She laughed. "Crazy, huh? You'd have to know my father to understand."

*I'll pass, thank you.* The words were on the tip of his tongue, but he bit them back.

Apparently his opinion showed on his face. Hands planted on her generous hips, she twisted her lips. "Don't go judging my daddy. That was just his nature. He couldn't help himself. Not everybody lives by your standards."

No safe response came to mind, so Thomas held his tongue.

"So tell me how you're feeling." She stepped in front of him and placed a hand on either shoulder, and then clucked her tongue. "Still all tensed up, I see. Well, come on back and we'll take care of that."

Shedding his shirt and shoes wasn't nearly as uncomfortable this time. The music and the trickle of water began their relaxing work even before Tuesday touched him. When she ran her hands across his back and immediately zeroed in on a bunched-up muscle, a sigh escaped his lips.

"It's amazing how you know exactly where the tight spots are," he said.

"Not really. A lot of people get knots in the rhomboids. And the trapezius too, of course."

"I don't know what those are, but I'm glad you do."

"I aced shoulder anatomy in massage school." He heard the smile in her voice. "It was my favorite course."

He lifted his head from the face cradle to peer over his shoulder at her. "I had no idea there were schools that teach massage."

"You thought we just put our hands on somebody and squeeze?" Her laughter filled the room. "Took me two years of hard work and a lot of money to get my certification as a massage therapist."

Her fingers slid upward and began working on his neck. Tension seeped away as the muscles beneath the base of his skull responded to her skilled touch.

"Do you have a degree?"

"Nah. I could have gone to a school where you earn an associate's degree, but what do I need with English and Algebra?"

Though he could have listed any number of reasons why a university education was helpful, at that moment she located a particularly sore knot in the place where his neck met his shoulder and the only sound he could manage was a sigh.

The conversation ceased as she continued to work. More relaxed than he could remember being, Thomas could easily have fallen asleep. In fact, his breathing became slow and deep, and a delicious drowsiness settled on him.

A loud clatter startled him fully awake. His eyes flew open and he looked over his shoulder to find Tuesday seated on her rolling stool, rubbing her knee.

"Doggone it. This room's so cramped I crashed into the table." With a final rub she reached for his foot. "I'll be so glad when I can get into my building and have room to spread out."

He settled himself again. "When will that be?"

"It's gonna be a while." She plied his foot with both hands and ordered, "Relax your toes."

With an effort, he did. "Why so long?"

"I have a lot to do. The building's real old. Needs painting and flooring and I have to put up a couple of partitions. Stuff like that. Plus the bathroom needs some work, and I don't know how to put in a toilet. Have to look it up on the Internet. I figure the whole thing will take me six months at least."

"You don't mean to say you intend to do the work yourself?"

"I have to. I can't afford to hire anyone." She finished with that foot and rolled sideways, her warm hands grasping the other. "That's okay. I'm not afraid of work. I just hope I can get clients to come here in the meantime."

Though Thomas applauded her attitude, the idea of a woman like Tuesday—who didn't look as though she would be particularly handy at renovations—doing major repair work struck him as ludicrous.

"Wouldn't it be more cost-effective to hire someone? A business location would hold far more appeal to your clientele than—a house." He started to say *than a run-down house,* but that would hardly be polite.

"Maybe, but I don't have the money. It took almost every cent my granny left me to make the down payment for the building. I have to save the little bit that's left so I have something to live on until I start getting customers."

"What about increasing your loan? Perhaps the bank would be willing to extend your line of credit."

"I asked, but they turned me down. Apparently they don't think a massage therapy business in Goose Creek has much potential. And I have such a great name, too." Her fingers deserted his foot, and he looked down to see her sketch a sign in the air. "*A Touch of Love.*" She smiled broadly. "Isn't that great?"

Thomas tried to imagine himself entering an establishment by that name. His lack of enthusiasm must have showed, because her smile faded.

"You don't like it."

"I am probably not your target audience."

"Sure you are. Everybody's my target audience." A grin appeared. "A man's money is as green as a woman's."

Obviously she had not spent a lot of time considering her business strategy. He could...but no. He had a big enough task ahead of him in switching jobs at the bank, selling his house, moving, and figuring out how to stop Susan from making a mistake that would have a disastrous impact on her future. Tuesday Love would have to make or break her business on her own.

"A good point," he answered. "And I insist that you let me pay you for today. You're selling a service. You'll never be successful if you give that service away for free."

"I totally agree, honey." She cocked her head sideways and awarded him a saucy wink. "And I won't turn down a tip, either."

Perhaps she would make a decent businesswoman after all.

# Chapter Nine

On Tuesday afternoon Al pulled his car down the long driveway of the house where he and Millie lived. He could not call it *home*, because this giant, hulking structure would never replace the comfortable place where they'd lived and raised their family together. No matter what Millie said, he would always think of this as the Updyke house, after the family that had built it more than a century ago and then unloaded it on him.

He parked beside her car in the wide space at the end of the crumbling driveway. No garage, of course. Yet another sacrifice he'd made for his wife. Come winter when they had to bundle up like Eskimos, brave the icy elements, and scrape frozen snow off of their windshields, she'd be sorry. For his part, he would swallow a thousand *I told you so*'s and suffer his lot in silence. At least, that was his intention now. When the time came and frostbite threatened, he might not be able to resist the occasional comment, just in case she didn't remember on her own.

The French doors leading from the dining room onto the porch—or verandah, as Millie insisted on calling it—opened, and his wife appeared in the doorway.

"Albert!" she called as he slid out from behind the wheel. "What are you doing home at two o'clock in the afternoon? Are you sick?"

Rufus bounded into the yard, barking his usual enthusiastic greet-ing. Al bent to deliver the expected pat on the head. Satisfied, the dog trotted back to the porch.

"I'm fine." Al closed the front car door and opened the back. "The more I thought about those squirrels, the less work I got done. Some-thing must be done."

"Justin is taking care of the attic. He's been up there all morning."

"I know that. I'm going to reclaim our yard. Give me a hand, would you?"

He pulled out a half-dozen shepherd's hooks and gave the rounded ends to her. "Let's take them over there, by the gazebo."

Rufus trotted beside her as she walked backward across the yard, carrying her half of their burden.

"Are you planning to do some landscaping?"

"No, these are for my birdfeeders."

She glanced at the empty feeders dangling from the wooden eaves of the gazebo.

"They're too easy for the squirrels to access there," he said before she could comment. "I might as well set out a pan of squirrel food and ring a dinner bell. But that stops today."

They deposited the hooks on the ground and returned to the car, where Al opened the trunk to display several twenty-five pound bags of birdseed.

Millie inspected the contents. "Goodness. You must have emptied the store's shelves. And what's that?"

"It's a squirrel trap." Al lifted out a wire cage and held it up for her inspection. "I don't know why I didn't think of searching the Inter-net before. These traps come highly recommended. They're easy to use, and they come in different sizes depending on the animal you want to catch."

A frown appeared on her face. "The poor squirrels won't be hurt, will they?"

Of course that would be his soft-hearted wife's primary concern.

"Not at all," he assured her. "The traps are completely humane. Here. Grab a couple."

He handed her a cage for each hand and carried four more across the yard himself. When those were deposited on the ground next to the hooks, they returned for a second load.

"Albert, how many traps did you get?"

He answered while giving her another pair. "Ten. I had to go to three stores."

When the cages had been piled on the ground, he stood back and surveyed the area. The grass grew thick here, surprising since shade from the tall, ancient trees cast a deep shadow over this entire part of the yard. He'd worked for a month to clear weeds from this one patch, and his efforts showed in a healthy blanket of lawn. Fifty yards away, at the back of the property, sunlight shone on the surface of the pond. One huge oak on the far end stooped low over the water's edge, and a stand of cattails grew at the opposite end.

Al placed a hand on the post of the gazebo and gave it a shake. Nice and solid. The porch swing inside was in decent shape too. Could use some sanding and a coat of sealant, but then it would be a nice place to sit on a lazy Sunday afternoon and watch the birds flit from feeder to feeder.

"I like it here," he said.

Delight lit her face. "You mean this house?"

"Definitely not." He glanced at the towering, multi-angled roof of the structure behind them. "I mean this part of the yard with the gazebo."

"Oh." Disappointment showed in the way her shoulders drooped. "Well, at least there's something you like about our home."

Her smile held a touch of false bravado, and an answering stab of guilt pricked Al's conscience. But he would not pretend to an attitude he did not hold. Why in the world was his wife so fond of that old house?

"Do you need help?" She swept her hand to include the materials piled around them. "I was just getting ready to put paint stripper on the staircase handrail."

"Go ahead." He scanned the tree branches above them through narrowed eyes. "I have an appointment with some pests."

When she headed toward the house, Rufus, who had been dozing in a patch of sunlight, leaped to his feet. He hesitated, his eyes going from Millie to Al, clearly torn. But in a contest between the two of them, there was no doubt of the outcome. He trotted inside after Millie.

After a mental survey of the area, Al laid out a plan.

❋

Ninety minutes later, Millie heard the back door bang shut.

"Millie, I'm finished. Come and see."

Setting her gooey scraper on a stained piece of newspaper, she descended the stairs and met Albert in the kitchen doorway. An eager spark danced in his eyes and his forehead—which was far more exposed than it used to be beneath a rapidly diminishing shock of gray hair—glowed bright red.

"You should have worn a hat." She placed a cool hand on his flushed skin. "You've got a sunburn."

"Never mind that. Come see what I've done."

He grabbed her hand and tugged. Trailing behind him, she couldn't help but grin at his enthusiasm. This was the first project about which he'd been truly eager since they left Mulberry Avenue. If only he'd tackle the minor repair jobs she assigned him with as much energy.

When she stepped out onto the verandah, her feet came to a halt on the flagstones. The sight before her was truly impressive.

Hideous, but impressive.

A double line of shepherd hooks protruded from the grass in the exact center of the open space, a birdfeeder dangling from each one. The base of each had been braced with a pile of large rocks and even a few bricks. Ugly wire cages had been positioned on the ground near every hook, and also at the foot of the four largest trees. A breeze blew the unmistakable odor of peanut butter in her direction. At her feet, Rufus lifted his nose and sniffed the air.

"It looks..." She grasped for a description. "Very effective."

"Oh, it'll be effective," he assured her. "Look at this."

She followed him into the yard and together they approached the nearest hook.

"These are six feet," he said, "too tall for a squirrel to jump from the ground."

Privately, Millie wondered if that were so. From the kitchen window she'd seen squirrels perform some impressive acrobatics.

Albert knelt and pointed out the iron rod. "I've coated them with cooking grease so the squirrels can't climb. And look inside the traps. Those are halved apples covered in peanut butter"—he grinned and finished with a note of triumph—"and sprinkled with birdseed."

"That would certainly tempt me if I were a squirrel."

Really, these cages scattered about made the place look like a junkyard. They quite spoiled the natural beauty of the lawn. Imagine what their guests would think if the B&B were open for business. She bit down on her lower lip and ventured a question. "How long will you leave the traps up?"

"As long as it takes." He shielded his eyes with a hand and scanned the treetops. "Since we have so many living here, it shouldn't be long before we catch a few."

A question came to mind, though she was almost afraid to ask. Hunters ate squirrels, didn't they? "What will you do with the ones you trap?"

"Release them on the far side of the county." A look of grim satisfaction settled on his face. "I'm thinking the mayor over in Morleyville needs some squirrels in his yard. That should make Jerry happy."

She was so relieved she didn't even chide him for the unkind thought.

※

Millie stood before the stove, browning hamburger for spaghetti. Through the kitchen window she kept an eye on Albert, who had not budged from the gazebo swing for the past hour. Once or twice she thought he might have fallen asleep, but his head did not nod. Instead, he watched the cages with the same intent stare of a cat stalking a mouse. Rufus, whom she had kicked out of the house half an hour ago to get some air, lay unmoving in the grass not far away.

A cardinal winged in to land on the far feeder and pecked at the seed. Well, that should make her husband happy, anyway. Nothing else seemed to lately. She smashed pink meat violently against the bottom of the skillet. Had she made a mistake convincing him to buy this house? She'd been so certain it was the right thing to do and that Albert would come around after they moved in. Instead, everything had gone wrong from the very beginning.

Unaccustomed to a melancholy mood, Millie brushed a bit of moisture from her cheek. Her deepest desire was to make a happy home for her family. When the children were little it had been so much easier. Make sure the chores got done and the kids got to ball practice and dance lessons on time, cook a family meal every night, oversee the homework. But now, the only "homework" they had was on a house that she loved and her husband tolerated. If only she could think of something to do to make him happy here.

Outside, the bird took flight. Albert heaved himself out of the swing and approached the house with a quick step. Millie brushed at her eyes and greeted him with a smile when he entered.

"I think I'm spooking them by sitting out there. I've seen a couple in the trees, but not a single one has come down to the ground."

"Then why don't you chop these peppers for me?" She pointed him toward the cutting board on the counter. "We can watch through the window."

He had no sooner picked up the knife when he jerked to attention, his gaze fixed on something outside. "Finally."

Coming to his side, Millie watched as a squirrel leaped from the trunk of one of the big trees, clearing the trap by several feet, and landed in the grass. It rose, tail twitching, and cocked its head sideways.

"It sees Rufus." Millie realized she was whispering, which was silly since they were inside.

"He doesn't see it." Annoyance colored Albert's tone. "That dog sleeps through everything except his supper."

The squirrel lowered to all fours and scampered across the yard to stop before the nearest wire cage. It inspected the opening, and even put its head inside.

"It smells the peanut butter," Albert said.

"There's another one over there." She pointed out a second squirrel making its cautious way toward one of the other traps.

Eyes gleaming, Albert turned a wide smile on her. He rubbed his hands briskly together. "We've got them now."

Squirrel number one stalked around the cage to the rear, nearest the bait. They watched as it reached through the wire grating in a vain attempt to get the apple.

Beside her, Albert chortled. "Do you think I'm stupid enough to put it where you can reach it, rodent? You have to go inside to get the food."

The second squirrel ignored the traps completely. It scurried to the base of a shepherd's hook and rose, eyeing the feeder suspended above its head.

"What's wrong with that one? The Internet said squirrels love apples." He rubbed his reddened forehead with a distracted gesture. "Maybe I should have gotten corn."

"Apparently it has a taste for birdseed," Millie said.

Al folded his arms. "Just try and get it, pest."

With no warning, the squirrel jumped. It landed on the pole about a foot and a half off the ground. Its front paws grasped the iron, and the creature dangled there for barely a second before sliding down to the ground.

Al shouted a triumphant "Ha!"

Undeterred, the animal leaped again, grappled for a hold, and again slipped down the pole. Retreating a few feet, it turned and surveyed the iron rod, tail twitching, before making a third attempt.

Chuckling, Millie watched as the poor squirrel clung with all fours only to slide again to the ground. "We should be videoing this for the grandkids."

Albert pointed, his rich laughter filling the kitchen. "Look, it's going to try a running start."

Sure enough, the squirrel darted backward several feet, turned, twitched its tail, and raced toward the pole. It managed to gain a height of almost three feet and wrapped all four paws tightly in a desperate attempt to stay in place. The inevitable downward slide sent both Albert and Millie into hysterical fits.

Squirrel number one abandoned its inspection of the trap and scuttled across the grass, coming to a stop not far from its cohort.

"He's gaining an audience," Millie managed to say between giggles.

"He's persistent, I'll give him that." Albert shook his head and wiped at his eyes.

Number two rubbed its front paws together with quick, jerky gestures, apparently trying to rid them of grease, and executed another impressive leap. Millie and Albert collapsed against each other, howling.

After a dozen or more attempts, the squirrel conceded defeat. With a final shake of its bushy tail, it sprinted across the grass, leaped onto a tree trunk, and disappeared in the canopy of leaves. Number one, apparently not willing to risk the same humiliation, followed closely behind.

Albert regained control of himself, though a wide grin remained on his face. At the sight Millie's heart lightened. It had been too long since they laughed together.

"I'm not giving up on the traps yet," he said, "but if I stock up on cooking grease, at least my feeders will be safe. Look."

The cardinal had returned, and this time she'd brought a friend. The two fluttered to a landing on either end of a birdhouse-shaped feeder and proceeded to enjoy a quiet meal.

"I'm glad." Millie slipped her arm around his waist. If she bided her time, the traps would disappear eventually.

They stood side by side watching the birds, when a sudden movement jerked Millie's gaze to the side. The squirrel had returned, but this time—

"I don't believe it." Albert placed both hands on the edge of the sink and leaned forward until his face was inches from the window. "That squirrel flew."

"Not flew," she said. "It jumped."

As they watched, a second squirrel dropped from the tree branches. It landed on the side of the nearby feeder and scrabbled for a hold while the container swung wildly and birdseed scattered. The two cardinals took off. A trio of new squirrels ran down a nearby tree trunk, descending in a normal way. They darted across the grass to take up positions beneath the hooks while the daredevils showered them from above with seed.

"Look at your dog." Albert pointed at Rufus, who had finally awakened.

His head came up and, after a quick look at the unusual activity in the yard, he leaped to his feet and bolted toward the house. A second later they heard a scratching and plaintive whine at the back door.

A flush spread across Albert's face, overtaking the sunburn and turning it purple. "That settles it. Tomorrow I'm ordering wildcat urine."

He stomped away before Millie recovered enough to reply.

# Chapter Ten

A knock sounded on Jerry's office door. He folded up the softball chart and slid it beneath a book on the edge of his desk. Just last night Cindie had accused him of being obsessed with this ballgame, and in a remote corner of his mind he feared she may be right. But every time he tried to tell himself *It's just a game,* Theo's smirk loomed large in his mind. If only he could wipe that arrogant expression off the man's face just one time.

*Pride goeth before a fall.*

Jerry squirmed in his desk chair. His grandmother used to quote that scripture. But it wasn't pride behind his desire to beat the pants off of Theo Fitzgerald. Was it?

"Come on in."

The door opened and two women marched into his office. Betty and Frieda. Sally followed the pair, wincing. *I tried to stop them,* she mouthed.

Nodding in her direction, he smiled at the women. These were, after all, his constituents.

"Good morning, ladies. Have a seat." He gestured to indicate the chairs opposite his desk. "What can I do for you?"

They settled themselves, Betty tucking her skirt demurely around her knees and Frieda blatantly hiking hers up to display more thigh than Jerry cared to see. He'd decided years ago that Frieda, a widow who lost her husband nearly two decades ago, didn't intentionally adopt a come-hither attitude. She was lonely, that was all.

Cindie disagreed, and strongly disapproved of the woman.

In the interest of marital harmony, he saw no need to mention today's meeting.

"We're not disturbing you, are we?" Frieda tilted her head to eye him sideways.

"Not at all." He flashed a quick smile in her direction, and then focused his attention on Betty. "What can I do for you ladies?"

"Well, we don't want to meddle." The older lady brushed at her skirt. "But we did wonder what all the secrecy was about."

"And we hope," added Frieda, "that we weren't the cause of any discomfort, since we were only offering constructive feedback."

His mind cast about for an explanation on which to anchor their comments. Coming up with none, he folded his hands on the desk in front of him. "I'm sorry. What are you talking about?"

Betty's eyebrows arched. "Why, the canopy, of course."

He blinked. "The canopy?"

Frieda leaned toward him. "At the water tower."

The tower again. Was this duo determined to stir up trouble? If he remembered correctly, they'd both been in favor of awarding the water tower painting job to Sandra Barnes.

After a moment of awkward silence during which Jerry felt that he should have been able to come up with a reasonable response, he flashed a quick smile at the ladies. "Why don't we take a walk?"

Betty dipped her head regally. "Yes, let's."

Clouds blocked the sun today, and they battled a fairly strong wind as they paraded up Main Street. Jerry looked upward and chided himself for not noticing the skeletal wooden structure circling the water tower earlier. When had it been erected? Two figures stood on the narrow platform, hammering.

Jerry and the ladies turned the corner of the Whistlestop Diner and approached the support legs of the tower. He cupped his hands around his mouth. "Hello up there."

The hammering ceased, and two faces appeared over the safety railing.

"Hello, Mayor," shouted Sandra.

"Hey," Little Norm added with a wave of his hammer.

At the risk of stating the obvious, Jerry waved a hand vaguely in the air. "What's going on?"

The two exchanged a glance, and then Sandra called, "We're coming down."

*Good.*

Jerry aimed a smile at Frieda and Betty, who stood off to one side and fixed expectant gazes on him.

Discomfort churned in his stomach. Busybodies or not, these two had every right to expect him, the mayor, to know what was going on in Goose Creek. The fact that he didn't left him shifting his weight from foot to foot and looking anywhere but their faces.

When Little Norm and Sandra had descended the alarmingly narrow ladder and stood on terra firma, Jerry fixed a smile on them. "What's up with the construction project?"

Frieda took a step forward. "There isn't much painting going on, even though that's what the city is *paying* for."

Little Norm, who was not little by anyone's standards, narrowed his eyes. "We're hiding our work, that's what. Gonna hang a canvas on this here frame to keep troublemakers from seein' what we're up to."

The ladies drew themselves up, and Jerry groaned.

Sandra answered before he could voice a response. "We're preparing a little surprise for the town."

That stopped Frieda, who cocked her head. "A surprise?"

With a loaded smile in Jerry's direction, the painter explained. "That's right. We're so proud of what we're doing we don't want to give it away. We want everyone in town to see it at once. *After* it's finished."

Betty and Frieda exchanged a glance.

"But then it'll be too late for our input." The whine in Betty's voice grated on Jerry's nerves.

Sandra's smile widened, and she stepped forward to put an arm around each of the ladies' shoulders. "You've given me valuable input already. And I sure do appreciate it." She turned them away and began walking toward Main Street. "Now I'm gonna give you two and this whole town a surprise that'll knock your socks off." Her Texas drawl faded as they disappeared around the corner of the Whistlestop.

Left standing beside Little Norm, Jerry stared after them. "That woman has a multitude of talents."

"Don't you know it?" Little Norm rounded on him, fists planted on his waist. "Those busybodies need to mind their own business and let us work. Having to hide ourselves behind a tent." He gestured angrily at the wooden frame being erected around the tower. "It's ridiculous, that's what it is."

Jerry stared after the women. Judging by the way Frieda and Betty had been led tamely away by Sandra, he doubted if he'd have any more trouble from them. She might even have gained a couple of supporters.

"But it's also a stroke of genius," he told Little Norm.

If only he could have a similar inspiration about the softball team.

※

When Al arrived home from work on Thursday afternoon, he made a quick tour of his traps. Not a single squirrel had taken his bait. All the cages sat exactly as he'd placed them, their insides empty of rodents but full of insects. The flies and ants certainly appreciated the feast of apples and peanut butter. The squirrel population was definitely not in danger of going hungry, either. Not a single seed remained in any of the feeders.

Tension buzzing in his ears, he headed for the house.

One of life's little enjoyments was walking into the house and being greeted by the aroma of dinner. His wife was, hands down, the best cook in the state. Nothing said *Welcome home!* like the smell of Millie's meatloaf or the spicy scent of her chili. And when she baked cookies, the mere fragrance of warm chocolate or sugary vanilla could lower his blood pressure by ten points.

Today, another odor greeted him when he entered through the kitchen door.

Coming to a halt inside, he wrinkled his nose. "What is that smell?"

"Mold killer." Millie appeared from the direction of the hallway, hair arranged and makeup freshly applied. "The men told me it wasn't dangerous, but I've got a headache from breathing it all afternoon."

Al gave an experimental sniff. "It's not bleach. Some sort of chemical, though, and it's kind of piney. Like floor cleaner."

"Don't even bother to put your car keys away." With a hand on his back she turned him around and gave a shove. "We're going out for dinner."

"But I've got to change clothes before practice," he protested.

"I have them here." She scooped up a bulging reusable grocery bag from the counter. "We're picking up Violet on the way to the Whistlestop. You can change at her house. Now let's get out of here before my brain pounds through my skull."

Since chicken and dumplings at the Whistlestop was a treat not to be argued with, Al allowed himself to be shoved through the door. Outside, Millie paused to fill her lungs with fresh air.

"Should we stay someplace else tonight?" he ventured. The cost of a hotel room was an expense not in his budget, but he'd sacrificed far more lately in the interest of marital harmony.

She shook her head. "Mold Man promised the odor would fade in a few hours. They've opened the windows and set fans upstairs and down. If it's still too strong when we get home, we'll sleep in the motorhome."

Al brightened at the idea. He glanced toward his RV, still parked at the far end of the driveway where it had been since they moved into this house. Once a week he started the engine and spent a few minutes in the driver's seat, staring through the windshield and planning the places they would one day visit. The Grand Canyon. Mount Rushmore. The Pacific Ocean.

That is, if the repairs to Millie's house didn't bankrupt them first.

※

Half the town had decided to visit the Whistlestop, it seemed. Al held the door open for Millie and Violet and scanned the interior. He exchanged a nod with Jacob Pulliam, seated with his wife at a table along the far wall.

"This place is fuller than a tick on a bird dog," Violet commented.

He did not bother to hide his distaste. "Couldn't you come up with something a little less distasteful right before we eat?"

She placed a finger on her cheek and cocked her head to consider. "Packed like sardines in a can, maybe?"

With a slow nod, he awarded his approval. "I like sardines."

"Look." Millie pointed across the room. "There's Susan and her father."

The pair sat in the center of a row of booths. Thomas, whom Al had met only twice, leaned across the table toward his daughter. He spoke quietly, and Susan gave an occasional nod but kept her gaze fixed on her hands, which were toying with a crumpled napkin.

"Oh dear." A concerned frown creased Millie's forehead. "She looks unhappy. I wish that man would give up this notion of moving to Goose Creek and go back to Paducah where he belongs."

Al raised his eyebrows. "What happened to your insistence that Goose Creek needs an influx of new residents?"

"We do, but not him." Her gaze fixed on someone else, and she bit her lower lip. "And I'm not sure we need her, either. The poor dear."

In one of the middle tables sat a woman alone, her attention fixed on a book. At one glance Al knew her identity. Millie had described Tuesday Love as a holdover from the sixties, and certainly the fringed blouse and wide headband lent her a retro appearance. But this woman was at least a decade younger than he and Millie, who had lived through enough of the sixties to recognize an authentic hippie.

"Is that the massage woman?" Violet inspected the stranger with unconcealed interest.

"Let's go speak to her. She looks lonely."

Millie and Violet threaded their way through the tables. Though unsure if he was to be included in the introduction, Al followed behind them. He had developed a great deal of curiosity about Goose Creek's newest resident. Several of the women had apparently taken a strong dislike to Ms. Love. Talk among the Creekers who gathered at Cardwell's soda fountain was performed in whispers, with many glances thrown over shoulders to ensure Lucy Cardwell didn't hear them discussing her and report back to their wives.

When they approached she caught sight of them. Her expression brightened and she snapped the book shut. "Millie! Good to see you."

She leaped out of her chair and hurried around the table to hug Millie as though they were long-lost friends. Conversations in the restaurant died as attentions were fixed on them.

Looking a bit flustered, and with more than a few glances around the room, Millie gave the woman's shoulder an awkward pat. "It's good to see you too." Her voice stretched thin, tone higher than usual. "This is my friend Violet, and my husband, Albert."

While the woman was busy shaking hands with Violet, Al shoved his into the safety of his pockets. Not only did he find shaking hands with women awkward—a holdover from the male-dominated culture in which he'd been raised—but he recognized the sound of jealousy in his wife's voice. After nearly forty years, he knew enough to maintain a polite distance when prudence called for it.

"Why don't y'all join me?" Tuesday gestured to the three empty chairs. "Seems a shame to take up two tables when the place is so busy."

Violet shook her head, and Millie said, "We couldn't intrude on your dinner."

"Please. I'd like the company." A plea appeared in her eyes. "I eat alone so much I'm starting to feel like a leper or something."

That decided his softhearted wife. Al watched Millie's expression go from reserved to compassionate.

"If you're sure you don't mind."

They arranged themselves around the table, Al selecting the chair at the opposite corner, as far from Tuesday as the limited space allowed.

The waiter arrived to take their orders, and Al didn't even glance at the menu before ordering his favorite meal.

When the young man left, Tuesday folded her hands on the table in front of her. "So how are my kitties?"

"You have cats?" Violet asked.

The woman giggled. "No, but I found a whole litter of them. I hope I'll be allowed to have one."

"You will," Millie told her. "Kate told me you could have the pick of the litter when they're old enough to leave their mother." She unfolded her napkin and asked without looking across the table, "How's the business coming along?"

Tuesday slumped against her chair back. "Slow. The building needs more work than I can afford. I've set up my table in my rental house, but so far I only have one client."

"You have one?" Violet's eyebrows arched, and she looked faintly scandalized.

"That's pretty good since you've only been here a week," Millie hurried to say.

"I guess. Back in Indianapolis I had lots of clients. They requested me all the time, and that made the center's owner mad. That's why I decided it was time to open up my own place." Her eyes flickered sideways, to somewhere behind Al's back. "But one client isn't gonna pay many bills."

Their drinks arrived then, and Al reached for a packet of sweetener from the bowl in the center of the table. "Maybe you should advertise."

"I'm trying. The newspaper only comes out once a week, and I missed the deadline. But I've got an ad in the next one. And I made up a sign for the front window of my new building." She squeezed lemon into her water and stirred with a straw. "I asked a couple of other places if I could put one in their windows, but..." She shrugged. "I guess they don't know me well enough yet."

"You mean they wouldn't let you hang a sign?" Millie asked.

"Oh, I don't blame them," Tuesday hurried to say. "I'm a stranger to town. They'll get friendlier soon."

Al exchanged a glance with Millie, who was still waging a similar war on behalf of her employer.

"Small towns don't take easily to newcomers," Violet ventured to say.

"I knew that." Tuesday straightened and put on a smile. "And especially when they're trying to introduce something new, like massage therapy. But that's one reason I picked this town. There's no competition within a forty-minute drive. All I have to do is get my hands on a person once and they'll come back." Her eyes flickered past Al again, and then settled on him. "How about you, Al? You ever had a massage?"

"Actually, yes."

Across the table Violet looked scandalized while Tuesday brightened. "Really?"

"Years ago when I was over in Nam. A few of my buddies and I went into Saigon on leave." The memory surfaced with vivid clarity. "One guy had been there before and knew all the bars that catered to American servicemen." He chuckled, warming to the tale. "I've never been so—"

Beneath the table, Millie pinched his leg so hard he jumped. Rubbing the spot that would certainly bruise by nightfall, he turned a reproachful glance on her.

"Our salads have arrived." She smiled brightly at the approaching waiter. "That was fast, even with this crowd."

Al deemed it the better part of wisdom to focus on his meal and forego any further discussion of his service days.

※

The napkin had become a damp wad in her hand. Susan smoothed it across her lap. Their meal had come and gone, though she had barely taken a bite. A nearly whole chicken sandwich, entombed in Styrofoam, rested on the plastic placemat before her.

Daddy recorded a tip and a total on the credit card receipt and signed in his careful script. Pocketing his pen, he slid the plastic check holder to the edge of the table. "Oh, and there's something I need you to do while I'm gone."

She tried not to look happy at the mention of his imminent departure, but the truth was, when Daddy went back to Paducah one major stressful element would be removed from her life. At least temporarily.

"What's that?"

"Keep an eye out for a suitable house. At least three bedrooms and preferably built within the past two decades, if such a thing exists here." He arranged his used silverware in the center of his empty plate. "My job situation may take a month or so to arrange, but if an opportunity arises before then we need to go ahead and act on it. The real estate market in this town isn't exactly robust."

Invisible bands squeezed Susan's chest, rendering her breath shallow. "About that. I'm not sure living together is a good idea."

Surprise colored his features. "Why on earth not? It's a logical arrangement based on our joint business venture and the finances involved." He leaned forward. "I'm not sure you realize this, but our house in Paducah has no mortgage. I paid it off long ago. And with property values being what they are in this town, I'll easily be able to buy something outright. It makes no sense whatsoever for you to continue paying rent for that tiny garage apartment when you can live rent-free with me."

In a way, Susan was pleased with the revelation. Daddy never discussed his personal finances with her, and doing so meant he finally considered her an adult. But her father's opinion of her maturity was not at issue here. Nor was the idea of free rent.

"It's just that I'm almost twenty-six years old. How many women my age do you know still living at home?"

"Are you worried about what others think?" He cocked his head.

"I'm surprised at you, Susan. You've never concerned yourself with the opinions of outsiders before."

"It's not that." The napkin once again became a tight ball in her fist. "I've grown used to being independent. Paying my own bills. Making my own decisions." She paused. "Spending my evenings however I wish."

He leaned back, resting against the booth's high back, and folded his arms across his chest. "You mean spending your evenings with Hinkle."

"If I want." She raised her chin and met his eye. "You might as well get used to the idea. Justin is my boyfriend." The word tumbled out awkwardly, like a middle school confession.

The air between them grew dense with Daddy's disapproval. "You're smarter than this, Susan. You deserve someone with at least as much intelligence and ambition as you."

Heat prickled beneath her collar. "Justin is intelligent. You'd see how smart he is if you would talk to him."

One corner of his mouth twitched downward. "He couldn't even finish college."

A waiter walked by, drawing her attention away from the two-foot space between them. Diners sat at nearly every table in the restaurant. Had her voice risen loud enough to be overheard?

She drew in a deliberate breath and released it slowly. "He left college because he knew what he wanted to do with his life, and he didn't need classes in Shakespeare in order to accomplish his goals. Which he *does* have."

That struck a note of some sort. Daddy's gaze flickered sideways for a second, a look of surprise on his face.

"We don't have time to discuss this anymore." Susan tossed the wad of napkin on her dirty plate and picked up her purse. "I have to stop by the apartment and get my tennis shoes before softball practice."

Returning a wave from Millie across the dining room, she left the restaurant. Daddy trailed behind her, silent for once.

# Chapter Eleven

Millie held Rufus's head while Susan looked in his ears. The poor dog trembled so badly she feared he might collapse of a heart attack right there on the clinic floor.

"What's the matter with you? You like Dr. Susan." She scratched the base of his tail, which normally sent him into fits of ecstasy, but his head only drooped further.

"I don't take it personally." Susan smoothed his ear down and switched to the other. "Some animals are afraid of the vet's office. His ears look fine." She put the earpieces of her stethoscope in place and pressed the drum against his chest. "Heart and lungs, too. He's perfectly healthy. How's his appetite?"

"Fine." Millie gave him an extra rub and then straightened when Susan did. Rufus immediately crossed the floor of the exam room and planted his nose in the door crack in a clear statement. "He eats well, but he doesn't have any energy. All he does is mope around."

Susan folded her arms and watched the dog with a thoughtful expression. "I think you're right. The move to a new house might have him a bit depressed. Dogs like Rufus who have been abandoned can be particularly sensitive to any change in their routine."

"Albert is the same," Millie said drily, "and he's never been abandoned."

"Change is never easy, especially for older people." Her eyes widened, and she put a hand out as if to retrieve the words. "Not that your husband is old. That's not what I meant."

Not offended in the least, Millie gave a quiet laugh. "Oh, but he is. Not old exactly, but Albert and I are certainly not spring chickens anymore. Still, even as a young man Albert resisted change."

"Just like my father." A troubled look appeared in the girl's eyes. "But sometimes change is necessary." She searched Millie's face. "Don't you agree?"

Though they'd become friends in the three months that they'd worked together, Susan rarely confided in her receptionist. Or in anyone, as far as Millie could tell, except her father and lately Justin. Still, Millie was attuned to nuances in relationships, and she'd have to be deaf and blind to miss the tension between Justin and Thomas Jeffries. Poor Susan was caught in the middle of two men she loved, never a comfortable position in which to find oneself.

In Millie's privately held opinion, Thomas's grip on his daughter went beyond that of a typical father. Probably because he'd lost his wife early and raised his daughter himself. Understandable, but the inevitable result of a tightfisted hold like that was a broken hand.

Millie filled her smile with compassion. "Absolutely. Change is inevitable. Sometimes it's even more painful for the person who forces a change than for those who resist it."

Susan gave her a sharp look. A moment later she nodded. "Well, anyway." Her tone became professional. "Give Rufus a little extra attention. He'll come around eventually."

"I hope so." Though Millie looked at Rufus, she was thinking of Albert.

※

When she and Rufus got home, good news awaited.

"You're mold free," declared Mold Man.

"Really?" So much had gone wrong lately she hardly dared to believe him. "Did you check the other rooms?"

"Sure did. Ran all the tests. Swabs. Samples. Air quality." He waved a hand in the air. "All came back clean. Even the basement looks good, though I'd recommend treating those concrete walls before too much longer as a preventative measure. Old basements are notorious breeding grounds for mildew."

"I will," she promised.

He laid a triplicate form on the kitchen counter and extracted a pen from his breast pocket. "Sign here."

She did, swallowing hard against the four-figure total at the bottom of the page. Albert would have a conniption. But what choice did they have?

When his truck had backed out of the driveway and disappeared from view, footsteps sounded on the stairs. Millie left the kitchen and arrived in the entry hall at the same time Justin stepped off the last step.

"They're finished." She waved her copy of the form. "Let's go see the damage."

Together they entered the parlor, and Millie winced at the sight of the giant hole in the wall beside the fireplace. Wooden posts rose from floor to ceiling, newly cleaned and free of the gray growth that had caused the sudden—and expensive—interruption to her plans.

Justin crossed the floor to inspect the beams closely. He shoved his head inside the jagged hole, squinting upward. "Looks good from here."

"From over here it looks ghastly."

He turned a sympathetic smile her way. "Don't worry. When I finish drywalling you won't be able to tell there was ever a problem."

She glanced around the beautiful room. The bay window, broken when they bought the house, had been replaced last month at a cost twice what she'd anticipated. Albert had thrown such a fit she'd decided to leave the renovation of the parlor until after at least two of the bedrooms—where paying customers would stay—were complete. But the discovery of mold had disrupted her plans. She couldn't leave a gigantic hole in the parlor wall, not when she planned to make this room the heart of their home. After the first upstairs bedroom was finished, this room would be where she and Violet concentrated their efforts.

Returning her attention to Justin, she studied him more closely. A hint of dark smudges marred the skin beneath his eyes, a telltale sign of sleepless nights that shouldn't trouble a healthy young man.

Unless he was in love.

While she must draw a line against prying into her employer's personal life, she had no such compunction about the young man before her. She'd grown to care about him over the past several months. "Are you feeling well?"

"Yeah. Well, mostly. " He raked fingers through his dark, curling hair. "I'll feel better come Sunday."

She knew without asking what would happen on Sunday. "That's when Susan's father returns to Paducah, isn't it?"

The look he gave her was sharp, and followed by a rueful smile. "Not much gets past you, does it, Mrs. Richardson?"

She answered with a small smile and watched him pace to the fireplace with long-legged steps.

"The trouble is, geography isn't going to change Mr. Jeffries's feelings." He laid a forearm across the ornately carved mantel and rested his head against it, staring with distant eyes at the marble hearth. "I've been as nice to him as I know how to be, but the man hates me."

"You know his feelings for you aren't personal, don't you?"

"You mean he'd feel the same about any man who's interested in Susan?" His lips twisted into a rueful line. "Yeah, I know. But he doesn't. He thinks I'm the cause of all his problems."

A particularly wise observation for a young man.

"But Susan loves you. Anyone with eyes in their head can see that. In the end, her opinion is the only one that matters."

"I know." Without raising his forehead from his arm, he turned toward her. The look on his face wrenched her heart. "But she's spent her whole life thinking her father is the smartest man in the world. And that he has her best interests at heart. When he moves here, it'll be a matter of time before she agrees with him."

Millie wanted to deny the dreadful prediction, but the words died unspoken. Thirty-seven years of marriage had taught her that a couple never really left the influence of their parents behind. Baggage, they called it. But a strong couple could carry the baggage, as long as they did it together.

"Then perhaps what's needed is a preemptive move."

He lifted his head, questions in his eyes. "What do you mean?"

Millie merely smiled. Albert often accused her of meddling without compunction, but that was untrue. She did draw the occasional line, and here was one.

"You'll come up with something," she assured him, and then changed the subject. "How's the attic coming along?"

He hefted himself away from the wall. "The squirrels have cleared out. I've covered all the grating with wire mesh and patched the holes. It's an obvious patch-job, though. At some point you'll probably want to do some restoration work on the original siding."

At what cost? When they bought the house, Millie had been furious with Albert for saying they would *repair* the house, but could not afford to *restore* it.

"That will have to come later," she said, "after the B&B starts making money."

"Well, at least all that carved trim hides the damage from anyone at ground level. And the trim is in good shape, as far as I could see."

"That's good anyway." She glanced in the direction of the backyard, where the ten traps still cluttered the lawn. "I don't suppose you could rid the yard of squirrels as easily as you cleaned out the attic?"

He heaved a laugh. "Can't help you there. Personally, I think Al's fighting a losing battle, but don't tell him I said so."

She certainly would not. If Albert heard that, he might decide to move into his travel trailer, and she'd never see him again.

❄

Al entered Cardwell's on Saturday morning, pleased to see a full contingent of Creekers once again. Saturdays in summer were some of his favorite days of the year. A quick scan of the crowd provided an extra mood-lifter—Thacker was not in evidence.

"Morning, manager," Fred called out.

"Morning, catcher," Al replied in a light tone as he claimed the stool vacated by Leonard Cardwell, who drained his coffee cup and headed for the pharmacy counter in the back.

Lucy picked up her husband's cup and replaced it with a full one for Al. He nodded his thanks and swiveled toward the tables, where Norman sat in one chair and his foot, swathed in a thick layer of Ace bandage, occupied another.

"How's the ankle?"

"Eh." Bushy eyebrows drew down to nearly obscure the older man's squinty eyes. "Hit pains me right bad. Doc won't gimme me no more pills, neither."

Beside him, Little Norm shook his head, disapproval heavy on the features that resembled his mother more than his father, thank goodness for him. "He doesn't want you to get addicted, Pa."

Lucy turned a scowl his way, her arms still elbow-deep in a sink full of soapy water. "You follow the doctor's advice. Don't mess around with pain pills."

"Bah!" He dismissed her with a wave and focused again on Al. "You'uns is doin' good, I hear. Gonna give them Morleyville fellers a run fer their money, ain't ye?"

Al caught Little Norm's eye, and the younger man quickly looked away. Apparently he'd been talking up the team's skills to his father, though why he would lie Al couldn't imagine. Probably to keep

Norman from hobbling onto the field to resume his place on the team. Well, Al wouldn't interfere.

"We're coming along," he said, and changed the subject. "How's the painting progressing?"

"Good." The word shot quickly out of Little Norm's mouth, and his lips clamped shut.

Beside him, Junior twisted in his chair. "What's with the tent, anyhow? Y'all got something to hide?"

Seated beside Al, Pete leaned sideways to fix a look on Little Norm. "Bill told me that woman ordered a load of paint from someplace down in Georgia."

"And what if we did?" Little Norm stiffened. "Sandra's used to working with a special kind of paint that you don't carry. She got all the basic stuff from you."

Clearly offended, Pete scrubbed at a drip of coffee on the counter. "I might have been able to order it."

"We hired her to do a job. Leave her alone and let her do it."

"So how come she's hiding her work?" Junior, apparently not ready to let the subject drop, planted an elbow on the table. "She ashamed of it?"

"No." Little Norm rounded on him. "We put that canvas up to keep the busybodies out of our business, that's why. Couldn't get any work done, what with having to stop and explain ourselves every ten minutes."

Surprise on his face, Junior shifted in his chair away from Little Norm. "Just askin', that's all. No call to get your drawers in a hitch."

With a visible effort, Little Norm replied in a calmer tone. "Everybody will see it soon enough. She's not only good, she's fast. Now that we can work in peace, the job's gonna be done earlier than we thought."

Usually Millie kept Al informed of all the happenings in Goose Creek, but she had not mentioned an accelerated reveal of the water tower. For once, he might have a bit of news to tell her. "When do you think you'll be finished?"

"We're aiming for the Fourth of July." With another stern look toward Junior, he picked up his soda. "That is, as long as nobody bothers us."

The door opened and, to Al's displeasure, Thacker bounded into the room. "Good morning, fellow Geese. *Honk, Honk.*" He put his hands in his armpits and flapped.

No one returned his special greeting, though several groans sounded from those gathered. Instead of taking offense, Thacker merely laughed, snorted, and headed for the far table. Woody caught Al's eye and quirked one eyebrow.

"Where's that fancy tablet of yours, Franklin?" Pete asked.

Wearing a surly expression, Lucy set coffee and the sugar bowl on the table in front of Thacker. Before he could comment, she shook a finger in his face. "Don't you dare call me 'sweet thang.'"

"Okey-dokey."

Jerking a satisfied nod, she turned away.

"Honey bun," Thacker added.

From where he sat, Al saw the scowl. Did Thacker realize how close he was to getting a cinnamon roll shoved up his nose? But with a visible effort and a hard set to her jaw, she returned to her place behind the counter.

"I left the tablet at home." Thacker spooned sugar into his coffee. "Apparently some people in this town are resistant to technology."

"That mean you've given up on your program?" Little Norm asked.

Thacker took his time answering. He finished stirring, set the spoon on the table, and picked up his mug. Raising it, he met Al's gaze. "Let's just say I'm working on another way to help the team."

He winked broadly, and Al found himself the object of several curious stares. He fidgeted on the stool and hid behind his coffee mug. Being aligned with Thacker left him distinctly uncomfortable. Whatever scheme the man had going now, he wanted no part of.

## Chapter Twelve

O kay, Suz, raise your glove. Watch the ball. This is going to be an easy one."

Her muscles so tight her arms trembled, Susan raised her glove above her head. As instructed, she stared at the ball in Justin's hand. Easy, since he stood only ten feet away.

He lowered his arm, knees bent, ready to toss the ball into the air for her to catch. Tension tightened in her stomach and she set her teeth.

Heaving a sigh, Justin straightened. "You've got to loosen up. You're going to end up getting hurt if you can't relax."

"That's what I'm afraid of." Fear made her voice sharper than she intended, and she immediately followed with an apologetic smile. "Sorry. But the game is only ten days away." Her tone descended into a wail. "I'm never going to be able to catch that stupid ball."

He stared at her a moment and then lowered his arm. "Let's take a break."

She followed him to the corner of the yard where a shaft of early evening sun still illuminated the green grass. Her landlords, the Hunsakers, kept their yard immaculate and encouraged Susan to relax there whenever she liked. Not that she had much free time, but it was nice to look out the window of her over-the-garage apartment on this small but peaceful patch of nature.

Justin indicated where she should sit and then lowered himself to the ground a few feet away. He sat cross-legged.

"Catch," he said, and tossed the ball.

So apparently their break wasn't for relaxing. Still, over a distance of a yard or so the ball didn't have a chance to gain frightening speed. She snagged it out of the air easily and tossed it back to him.

"There you go." His encouraging smile warmed a bit of the chill in her stomach, even though it was ridiculous to take pride in catching a ball that a toddler could handle. "Tell me about that soccer ball incident. How old were you?"

"Oh, seven or eight. I was at school in gym class, and Rodney Blair kicked it straight at my face." She caught the ball again. "I think he did it on purpose."

"He probably had a crush on you. Boys are weird like that."

She tilted her head and asked, "Did you ever kick a soccer ball at a girl you liked?"

"No." A wide grin appeared. "But I did cut the curls off of Angie Fricker's hair in fifth grade. She sat in front of me."

"Meanie." She lobbed the ball with a little more force, smiling.

"Use your glove to catch this one," he said. "So you lost three teeth?"

The next ball dropped into her open glove thanks more to his aim than any ability on her part. "Yeah. The dentist reimplanted two of them but this one"—she tapped on a tooth—"is a crown."

"Can't tell at all. Must have been pretty traumatic, huh?"

"I remember there being a lot of blood." She shuddered. "They took me to the nurse's station and called Daddy. He got me to the dentist within an hour, which is the only reason they were able to save any of them."

The ball ping-ponged between them a few times.

"Your dad's been there for you a bunch." Justin's gaze remained fixed on the ball.

"Always," she said quietly.

"I can't imagine how hard this must be for you."

The tenderness in his voice reached inside her conflicted thoughts and left her fighting tears.

He tore up a few blades of grass and tossed them aside. "If you want me to back away, give the word."

Startled, she looked up into his face. "Do you want to?"

"What do you think?"

For a moment, his eyes opened a pathway through which she saw his heart. Longing. Sadness. Desire. But above all, a tender love that threatened to rob her of breath. She launched forward on her knees, rested her hands in the grass between them, and planted a kiss on his lips.

When she backed away, a wide grin appeared on his face. "Then I'll just have to win him over with my charming personality."

Then he tossed the ball into the air. Not far, but high enough to arc over the space between them and descend toward her. Without thinking, she grabbed it out of the air.

"You did it!" His shout rang throughout the yard.

"That doesn't count." She scowled at the ball resting in her glove. "You're only three feet away."

"It's the same thing," he insisted. "You just watch the ball, put your-self beneath it, and let it fall into your glove."

Though she knew the difference between the velocity of a ball tossed from three feet away and one flying toward right field from the batter's box, a jolt of triumph shot through her. Maybe, with Justin's help, she really could break free from this fear.

Maybe she could break free from several things.

※

The sound of the front door opening reached Jerry as he pulled a tray of baked chicken out of the oven.

"I'm home, Jer," Cindie called from the living room. "Supper smells great, whatever it is."

He set the hot tray on a trivet and, tossing the oven mitt on the counter, went into the living room to greet his wife. Cindie set her purse and briefcase on the couch and entered his arms for a hello hug. Like many Goose Creek residents she commuted forty minutes each way to a job in Lexington. As a result, Jerry usually got home long before she arrived.

"The potatoes are almost ready," he told her. "We can go ahead and start on the salad."

"Sounds good."

They headed for the kitchen but were interrupted by Jerry's cell phone. He lifted it from the counter and glanced at the screen. "Paul Simpson. I wonder what he wants." Pressing the button to answer, he propped the phone on his shoulder and removed a green salad from the fridge. "Hey, Paul."

"Mayor, there's trouble at the tower. You'd better get over there quick."

Scowling, he set the bowl on the table. Cindie raised her eyebrows in a question.

"Don't tell me Betty and Frieda are at it again," he said into the phone.

Cindie rolled her eyes.

"Nah, it's not them. It's Junior."

That drew him up short. "Junior? What's he doing there?"

"Wait, I think that's the ambulance. Gotta run."

Jerry jerked upright. "Ambulance?"

The call disconnected. Wide-eyed, Cindie asked, "Something's happened to Junior?"

"I don't know, but I'd better get over there."

"I'm coming with you."

She grabbed a piece of foil to cover the chicken while he turned off the fire beneath the potatoes. Snatching his keys, they hurried to the car for the two-minute drive down Maple Avenue.

A small crowd had gathered a short distance from the base of the tower. An ambulance had been pulled all the way to the edge of the gravel drive, red lights flashing, and two EMTs knelt beside Junior's supine figure.

When Jerry jumped out of his car, Paul detached himself from the onlookers and joined him in hurrying to Junior's side.

"What happened?"

"Don't know. I'd just parked my car in front of the diner and was getting ready to go inside when I heard him hollering. Found him lying on the ground, moaning. I called the ambulance first and you second."

"Thanks, Paul."

They arrived at Junior's side. One of the paramedics knelt at Junior's head, holding it with both hands, while the other snapped a cervical collar around his neck.

With a nod at the closest one, Jerry lowered himself to his haunches a couple of feet away. "Junior, are you okay?"

"Oww." He opened his eyes, and then squinted them shut. "It hurts a heap, mayor. Cain't hardly move a'tall."

"What happened? Was it a wreck?" He glanced around the immediate area. No sign of Junior's pickup.

"He fell off the tower." The paramedic pointed to the steel rungs rising from the ground to the platform high above.

Good heavens, had the man broken his neck? "Is he going to be all right?"

"He'll be fine." The second paramedic finished his work with the collar and stood. "He was only a few feet off the ground."

"My boot slipped plumb off the ladder," Junior moaned.

Jerry glanced at his footwear. Yes, the same work boots he insisted on wearing to softball practice.

"Apparently he fell on his arm." The paramedic beside Junior pointed to the swathed arm brace. "It's for a doctor to say, but I think it's broken."

"Oooooooohh," Junior moaned.

Paul, standing a few feet away, ventured a question. "Why do you have his head immobilized like that?"

"Just a precaution," the paramedic assured him.

"Junior, what were you doing up there?" Though why Jerry bothered to ask the question, he didn't know. The answer was obvious.

"I jes' wanted to see the picture, that's all. They's bein' so hush-hush about it, like it's some kind of big secret, made me wanna see."

Jerry bit back a comment about curiosity and what it did to cats. On the other hand, cats landed on their feet, whereas Junior apparently hadn't mastered that skill.

When the ambulance pulled away, Jerry stood with the small group of onlookers watching until the red lights disappeared around the corner of the Whistlestop. There went his shortstop. Not that Junior was a good shortstop by any means, but even a bad player was better than being a man short. The game was in ten days. Unless he could find a replacement, and fast, he'd have to forfeit.

Cindie stepped up to his side. "I'll play."

Not bothering to hide his surprise, he turned toward her. "But you hate softball."

"Yes," she nodded, "but I love you."

He slid an arm around her waist and hugged. "Thank you."

"But do me a favor," she added. "Put me someplace that won't see much action. And keep looking for someone else." She lowered her voice. "I'm probably not even as good as Dr. Susan."

"I will."

Though he fully intended to make good on his promise, he didn't hold out much hope of success. He'd already called everyone in town.

❊

"Well, look at you. I didn't expect to ever see you again after you went home to Paducah."

Wincing at the volume of Tuesday's enthusiastic greeting, Thomas glanced at the surrounding yards. In truth, he was more surprised than she to find himself standing on her lopsided front porch.

"My departure was temporary," he told her. "But I still spend my weekends here in Goose Creek. I thought if you have some free time..." He craned his neck to peek behind her.

The full lips twisted into a sarcastic grimace. "Honey, I've got time, but it isn't free. Come on in."

He edged past her into the small living room. Not a box in sight, and the addition of a couple of table lamps, a quilt, and several brightly colored throw pillows had transformed the room into a comfortable, if somewhat confined, space.

"Has business picked up?"

"Not at all." A troubled expression overtook her normally cheerful countenance. "If I didn't know better, I'd think some of the ladies in this town had blackballed me."

"What makes you think so?"

"Oh. You know." She plucked at a curl dangling at her temple, an escapee from her headband. "Sideways looks they give me. The tail end of whispers I overhear."

Though Thomas's exposure to the female gender was admittedly limited, he was no stranger to the quirks and cliques of small towns. His own daughter had fought a similar battle when she moved to Goose Creek earlier this year. Though she'd achieved a grudging acceptance, she was still considered an outsider, and no doubt would be for a good time to come.

"Don't give up," he advised. "Given time, they'll come around."

"I hope so." Then she brightened. "What are we standing here for? Go take those clothes off so I can get my hands on you."

Sometimes her choice of words left him feeling a little uncomfortable.

In the massage room he removed his shirt and shoes and considered her problem. If she uttered questionable comments such as the one she'd just delivered in the company of conservative women, no wonder they'd taken a dislike to her. Tuesday Love was her own worst enemy.

"Ready in there?" she called.

He settled his face in the cradle and sighed, anticipating the treatment he was about to receive and tonight's subsequent restful sleep. "Ready."

Her fingers began their magical movements on his back, and he sighed, tension leaching out of his body by the second.

"How is work on the building coming?"

"Slow." She traced his spine and located a tender place about mid-back. "I picked out some paint, but when I put it on the wall it looked like dog barf."

Trying to picture that went beyond his imaginative abilities, thankfully. "I still think you should go back to your bank. With a solid business plan and some market research, maybe they'll reverse their decision."

"See, that's where you lose me." She set to work on his shoulder with her expert touch. "I probably would have learned stuff like that if I'd gone to college, huh? I wouldn't know where to start."

Perhaps it was the result of his extreme enjoyment of the massage. Before he could censor his words, he volunteered. "It wouldn't be difficult. I could help."

Her hands halted. "Would you really?"

Thomas could have bitten his tongue. What was he thinking with an offer like that? Didn't he have enough to do already, what with trying to convince the bank president to move him to Lexington and helping to ensure his and Susan's business venture stayed her top priority?

But the offer was made and, judging by the unmasked hope in her voice, highly appreciated. Retreating now would make him nothing more than a brute. Besides, he meant what he said. Conducting a small amount of market research wouldn't take much time. And she could do a lot of the legwork. Should, in fact, since she knew the business aspect of her profession better than he did.

"Certainly. It's a simple matter of defining your customer base, studying on their demographics, and then formulating an approach that appeals to them. And recording the information in a business plan, of course."

"You can do all that?" A note of enthusiasm crept into her voice.

"Easily," he assured her. "I do work for a bank, after all."

"That's right." She giggled. "You do."

When she got to his feet, she exclaimed, "Thomas! Your toes are all crunched up again." *Tsking*, she tackled his right foot. "Have you had a lot of stress in the past couple of weeks?"

Her kneading produced a sigh, half-painful, half-pleasurable. "You have no idea."

As if it weren't enough that the realtor delivered a dismal price on the value of his home, the bank's directors were unconvinced that relocating an executive to the Lexington branch was an advantageous move. As his feet relaxed his tongue did the same, and before he knew it the whole story poured out.

"So as it stands now, I'll have to either accept a demotion and a significant cut in my pay and bonus opportunities or find a comparable position with another bank."

"Your toes are clenching again." She rapped them with a finger and continued massaging when he forced them to relax. "So are you sure this is what you want to do?"

"I have one daughter," he replied, "and she needs me. I can't help her from two hundred miles away."

"Susan seems like a pretty together girl to me."

He did not reply, and she worked for a moment in silence.

"I'll be glad to have you close, since you're my only customer." Another giggle, and the sound marked the close to the uncomfortable topic.

"We'll soon take care of that. Together," he added, lest she get the impression he would do the work alone.

"Together," she agreed. "Sort of like partners. You know the boring business stuff, and I know the fun stuff. We'll make a great team."

He could have voiced a ready answer, but her words echoed another conversation he'd had not long ago. A disturbing parallel drew itself in his mind.

"Hey, since we're going to be partners, we ought to share the profits, huh?"

The comment drew his attention sharply back. What was the woman going on about now?

"I won't accept payment, so don't even think about suggesting it."

"I wasn't talking about money." She stood from her rolling stool and gave his foot a final pat. "Since you'll be here in town, how about free massages for life?"

His arms felt like limp ribbons, his feet like a cool drink of water on a summer day.

"You've got a deal," he said.

※

Late Saturday morning, Al bid the Creekers goodbye and crossed the train tracks in front of Cardwell Drugstore. Only a few days of June remained, and the Weather Channel's promise of a hot, dry summer had proven true. The sun had baked the inside of his car to an oven-worthy temperature, and he lowered all four windows before pulling away from the curb. The fact that he had to drive to his favorite hangout on Saturdays still irritated him. For years he had enjoyed the four-block stroll downtown from the house on Mulberry Avenue, the place he still thought of as home. The Updyke house lay a couple of miles down Ash Street, one of the last structures inside the Goose Creek town boundary in that direction. Though Millie insisted the exercise would do him good, he knew better than to walk on hot summer days. If he didn't collapse from heat exhaustion, he'd probably get run over by one of those crazy teenaged drivers.

On a positive note, his wife rarely suggested that he drag Rufus along with him these days. At least he was spared cleaning a pound or two of dog hair off of his cloth car seats.

While driving down Walnut Street, he gave in to an impulse and executed a quick left turn onto Mulberry. For nearly two months he had avoided passing the old place. Far better to relish the pleasant memories than to torture himself with the sight of Thacker's car in *his* driveway and Thacker's name on *his* mailbox. But Violet's comment a few weeks ago refused to be banished from his mind. What had the man done to the backyard? Maybe he'd be able to glimpse the damage from the road.

He drove slowly, relishing the familiar sight of neat, square yards lining both sides of the street. The houses all lay a uniform fifty-three feet from the sidewalk, their driveways smooth and unadorned with weeds growing through cracks in the blacktop. His eyes were drawn to the most beautiful lawn on the street, located in the exact center on the right side.

A flash of plaid caught his eye. A man wearing red, white, and blue Bermuda shorts stood on the walkway leading from the sidewalk to the front door of his former home. Drat. Not only was Thacker home, he was outside. Al tapped the brakes and the car slowed. Should he turn around? Or zoom past? Thacker faced the house, his back to the street, so maybe he wouldn't notice a car driving behind him.

His attention was focused on a task. What was he doing? As Al watched, he planted a shovel in the ground and jumped on it. He pushed on the handle a few times and then repositioned the blade. When he reached down and grabbed a plant, Al stomped on the gas pedal. The car shot forward, and when he arrived at his old house he slammed on the brakes, still in the middle of the street.

"Here now, what are you doing with that camelia?" He did not bother to filter the anger from his shout.

Thacker turned, his expression clearing when he recognized Al. "Bert! Good to see you, buddy." He held the uprooted plant aloft. "I'm getting rid of these old bushes. The wife's got her heart set on petunias."

Al shoved the gearshift into park and leaped out of the car. "You can't do that. Those are healthy bushes. You can't just dig them up."

"Healthy?" Thacker blew a blast through pursed lips. "Look at 'em. The flowers were beautiful a week or two ago, but now they're all wilted. We must have done something wrong, because they're all dying."

"They're not dead, you—" He stopped himself before the word *idiot* emerged. Thacker's eyebrows arched, and Al lowered his volume. "They're not dead. They bloom in the spring, and then the flowers drop off. They're beautiful green shrubs."

"Huh?" Thacker inspected the plant, and then shrugged. "Well, we don't like them." He tossed the butchered bush into the grass.

Mouth gaping, Al could not pull his gaze from the camelia, which sprawled there, surrounded by dandelions—*Dandelions!* In *his* yard!— like a murder victim.

"Having a little trouble letting go of this place, are you, Bert?" Thacker dusted his hands on his ridiculous shorts. "You need something else to think about. Like the big game. It's in nine days, you know. Just three more practices. Now, I've been working on my analysis, and...Bert?" He snapped his fingers a few inches from Al's nose. "You still with me, Bert?"

A rush of memories played in Al's mind. David and Doug had come down from Cincinnati to help him plant those camelias. Millie used to sit on the front porch and talk to him while he trimmed them to perfect roundness. They'd taken snapshots of the grandkids standing on this very walkway while bright pink blossoms covered every plant.

He tore his gaze away and fixed it on Thacker. The sad truth was that this man, this *idiot*, had bought his camelias along with the house. If he wanted to dig them up and discard them, he had every right.

Rendered speechless, he turned away from Thacker.

"Hey, where are you going? I wanted to tell you what I've been working on."

If he opened his mouth, he'd say something he might one day regret. Instead, Al opened the door and slid behind the wheel. He put the car in gear and drove away without a backward glance.

❋

"It was a mistake to go there." Albert slumped in a chair at the kitchen table. "I only wanted to see the old place, but now it's worse than ever."

Millie's heart twinged. Poor Albert looked so despondent.

She reached for his hand and intertwined her fingers in his. "I'm sorry."

A huge sigh. "It's not your fault."

But the fault did lie with her. She meant the apology to cover a multitude of hurts. Sorry for his sadness. Sorry for his camelias, of which he'd been so proud. Sorry for insisting they sell the house on Mulberry Avenue to the Thackers, even though Albert clearly detested his odious coworker. Sorry for uprooting him from the home he loved and dragging him to one in which he was obviously miserable. At times like this guilt churned in her stomach. She really had thought he would come to love this house once they moved in.

Now that they lived here, her vision of the beautiful bed and breakfast seemed like a pipe dream, a distant and increasingly unattainable fantasy. The costs of unanticipated repairs like mold and squirrel elimination were mounting. She was not afraid to work and had promised to do much of the decorating herself to cut costs. But her sixty-something-year-old body didn't bounce back like it had thirty years ago. Or even ten years ago. Her muscles ached from stripping wallpaper and scraping paint. And there was so much more to do. The number of tasks to be accomplished increased daily, and at times they piled so high they blocked her view of the goal at the end—a beautiful bed and breakfast that was not only charming and comfortable, but profitable enough to satisfy Albert.

But what could be done about the situation now? They'd committed themselves and a significant amount of their retirement income. Even if she'd made a mistake—which she still wasn't prepared to accept—they had no choice but to plow ahead.

"You know what we've got to do?" She squeezed Albert's hand and forced a smile. "We've got to be like the pigs."

The despondency left his face, replaced by a look of such confusion that she couldn't help a chuckle.

"I beg your pardon?" He made a show of squinting his eyes and peering closely at her. "I think I need to clean out my ears. I thought you just said we need to eat like pigs."

"Not eat like pigs." She cocked her head, a thought occurring to her. "Though Roberta Tolliver does swear that chocolate ice cream makes her feel better whenever her son loses another job and moves back home."

A hopeful look appeared on Albert's face. "Do we have any ice cream?"

"No." Millie squeezed his hand. "What I said was we need to *be* like pigs. They have no necks, so they can't look back. Only forward. That's why you're supposed to eat pork on New Year's, so you can put the past behind you and anticipate the future."

For a moment he said nothing. Then the hint of a smile stole over his lips. "Do you know what I love about you, Mildred Richardson? You're a Pollyanna. Always looking on the bright side of things."

"I have to, since I live with Eeyore."

"Did you just call me a...donkey?"

"A very lovable one," she assured him.

That brought a laugh, and the sound lifted Millie's spirits considerably.

"Speaking of pigs." Albert looked toward the refrigerator. "Do we have any ham? I'm starving."

"No ham, but I have some really good egg salad. How about a sandwich?" At his nod, she rose and began assembling the ingredients of their lunch.

Albert washed his hands at the sink, staring into the backyard. "The wildcat urine isn't working, is it?"

Carrying a container of egg salad, she came to his side. Outside a pair of squirrels scampered across the lawn, probably searching for any birdseed they'd left behind when they emptied the feeders yesterday.

"It doesn't seem to repel the squirrels," she admitted, "but it has certainly kept Rufus out of the backyard. I have to take him through the front door when he needs to go out."

At the mention of his name, Rufus's ears perked up.

"For once, I don't blame him," Albert said. "Our backyard stinks."

Millie wrinkled her nose, relieved that the observation had come from Albert instead of her complaining about his latest attempt to rid the property of squirrels. "It positively reeks," she agreed.

"I've caught only two of the pesky things in my traps. Greasing the poles doesn't work. I'm out of ideas." He gave her a sour look. "I may have to concede defeat, like Rufus."

Now that his mood had brightened, Millie couldn't stand watching the despondent Albert return. "I have an idea." She spread egg salad on whole wheat bread. "After lunch let's go downtown and get some ice cream."

The suggestion worked. He slipped an arm around her and gave her waist an appreciative squeeze. "I'll have chocolate."

"You know what?" She grinned up at him. "So will I."

# Millie's Healthy Egg Salad

2 eggs
⅓ to ½ cup low fat or fat free cottage cheese
¼ tsp mustard
Scant ¼ cup diced dill pickle (optional)
Salt and pepper to taste

Place eggs in a small pan and cover with water. Bring to a rolling boil. Put a lid on the pan and turn off the burner. Let the eggs sit for 20 minutes, and then cool before peeling. Chop the eggs in a small bowl. Use the tines of a fork to smash up the larger pieces of cooked egg white. Mix in the remaining ingredients, using enough cottage cheese to achieve the desired consistency. Serve on whole wheat bread or wrap with a crisp lettuce leaf. Makes two hearty sandwiches.

# Chapter Thirteen

The telephone on Al's desk rang. Fighting a flash of irritation at the interruption, he finished keying a line of code before snatching up the receiver. "Richardson here."

"Hey Al. It's Jerry. Got a minute to talk about softball?"

A mental gear shift occurred. Al extracted himself from his work and donned a different hat, this one a ball cap. "Sure. Everything all right?"

"I think the real question is, is anything all right?" A heavy sigh sounded through the phone.

Though Jerry was one of the most even-keeled men Al knew, it had become obvious to just about everyone that he was preoccupied with this game. He'd made no secret of his desire to defeat Morleyville's team, and especially Morleyville's mayor. But Cindie had confided to Millie that Jerry wasn't sleeping well. A few days ago he'd woken her up at three in the morning shouting, "Tag him before he touches the base!"

"It's not that bad," Al told him. "It's only a game, Jerry."

"Right." A brief pause. "I'm going over the plan for tonight's practice. Maybe we should shift some positions around. What do you think of moving Alice to shortstop and Paul to third?"

Why in the world would the mayor ask *his* opinion? So far Al's only task for the team was to bring the equipment to each game, make sure everybody lined up in the correct batting order, and take the equipment home when practice ended.

"What does Justin say?" he asked.

"He thinks it's too late to switch people around."

"I agree with him," Al said. "We only have two more practices before the game, tonight and Saturday. I think we should keep everybody where they're comfortable."

"What if we call extra practices? We could fit one in tomorrow night, and maybe Sunday afternoon too."

Al grabbed a pen from his desk and rocked back in his chair. "If you want my opinion, that's a bad idea. People are having fun. Well, most of them are." He thought of Dr. Susan, who still looked like she was going to faint whenever a ball headed toward right field, and Alice, who had to find someone to keep an eye on her brood during every practice. Cindie had watched them a couple of times, but now that she was playing, Millie and Violet teamed up to babysit. Even Millie, who loved children, had a few harsh words for the Wainright boys' wild ways. "If you push too hard, you'll take the fun out of it."

"But we have to do something." Jerry continued the lowered voice of one confiding a secret. "I just hung up the phone from Theo Fitzgerald. He tried to talk me into wagering a hundred bucks on the game."

"Did you do it?"

"No. The voters would roast us both alive if they found out. Still, he must be pretty confident to suggest such a bet."

"Must be," Al agreed. "But who cares?"

Another loud breath. "You're right. So what if we lose? I've tolerated Theo's stuck-up attitude for years. I guess I can put up with a few months of bragging too."

Someone entered the mayor's office for an afternoon meeting, and they ended their call. Al replaced the phone and stared at it a moment before returning to his computer. At least Jerry had the sense not to take that bet. This started out being a friendly inter-county ballgame, a pleasant way to pass the time on the Fourth of July. Putting money on the outcome would elevate it to something far less neighborly.

Still, it would be nice to win.

A head popped up over the top of Al's cubicle wall. Thacker peered at him suspiciously. "Were you listening to my phone call?"

Al drew himself up. "Certainly not." Then he narrowed his eyes. "Were you listening to mine?"

"Nope."

Thacker disappeared, and within a few seconds the sound of computer keys tapping emanated from his cubicle.

Tossing his pen on the desk, Al returned to work.

❄

"There." Millie straightened a wrinkle from the bedspread and stepped back.

Violet nodded her approval. "This room's pretty as a picture."

Millie cast an admiring gaze around the upstairs bedroom. As Justin had promised, the hole where the mold treatment was applied showed no sign of the destruction done to the wall. Removing all that busy wallpaper had given the room a spacious, open feel. She'd feared the sky blue color would be overwhelming, but it created a refreshing, outdoorsy atmosphere that made her want to throw her arms wide and whirl like a child in a field. The old poster bed left behind by the Updykes had cleaned up beautifully, and with the new mattress and bedding it gave the room just the right blend of antique and modern comfort. In the corner near a chest of drawers stood the rocking chair from their former living room with a new seat cushion that matched the comforter.

She eyed the bed. "Maybe another decorative pillow or two."

Violet disagreed. "Leave well enough alone. A guest will be snug as a bug in a rug in here. After all, all work and no play makes Jack a dull boy."

Millie shook her head. Sometimes Violet got carried away with her sayings. "That last one doesn't fit."

"It certainly does." Violet raised her nose in the air. "It applies to you. You've worked too hard, and you need time off to rest. Don't undertake another task until after the holiday."

"The Fourth of July isn't for another five days. I can probably have the staircase railing finished by then."

"Leave it," her friend advised. "It won't grow legs and run away."

"Well..." Millie brightened. "Albert's off for the long weekend. I could help him in the yard. Oh, that reminds me. I wanted to ask you—" Enthusiastic barking echoed up the stairs from below. Millie glanced at her watch. "Goodness, look at the time. He's home already." She went to the landing at the top of the stairs. "Albert! We're upstairs. Come up and look at the guest bedroom."

He entered the entry hall with Rufus trotting at his heels. "Have you finished it?"

"Yes indeed. Come and tell us what you think."

When he headed up the stairs, Rufus bounded ahead of him like a pup. Millie bent down to rub his ears, and his tail wagged with energy. She hadn't seen him display this much spirit in months.

"Are you feeling better today?" she asked the dog, and when Albert joined her, "And how about you? How was your day?"

His lips twisted into a mock-disapproving line. "You check with the dog before your husband? I see how it is. I've been replaced in your affections." He affected an insulted expression and even went so far as to give a fake sniff.

"Never." She kissed his cheek, reveling in his playful mood. This side of Albert didn't appear often, but she immensely enjoyed the times when it did. She took his arm and tugged him toward the front bedroom. "I can't wait to show you."

In the past week and a half she had refused to let him in the room, insisting that she wanted to surprise him with the finished product.

"Should I close my eyes?" he asked.

"Just come on, silly."

She led him to the room and Violet stepped out of the way to give him a clear view. His head moved as he inspected the area.

"Nice." Crossing the floor, he ran a hand over the wall where the repair work had taken place. "Very nice." When his gaze fell on the comforter, a slight frown appeared. "I don't remember that. Is it new?"

"Yes." When his frown threatened to deepen, she rushed on. "I got it on the sale rack at Walmart. They were practically giving it away."

"Hmm." He cocked his head, and then nodded. "It looks nice. The whole room does." He turned to include Violet in his praise. "You two have done a fantastic job. Any bed and breakfast guest would be lucky to stay in this room."

Millie and Violet shared a preening grin, and then she crossed the room to open a door on the opposite wall. "Only this bathroom isn't ready for guests yet."

Al inspected the tiny space. "What's wrong with it?"

"Nothing's *wrong* with it. Everything works, but it's rather austere. I'd like to replace that pedestal sink with a vanity, and the mirror's cracked in one corner. But after spending so much on Mold Man's bill, I don't want to spend any more money on this room yet."

Though he gave her a look of approval when she mentioned not spending money, he shrugged. "So rent it to a man. Guys don't care about stuff like that."

He went still. An odd look came over him, as if he'd noticed something astonishing. Millie glanced at the corner where he stared, but nothing looked amiss.

"Albert? Is something wrong?"

Eyes wide, he hissed in a breath. "Why didn't we think of this before?"

Millie exchanged a glance with Violet. "Think of what?"

"I have to make a phone call." He whirled and brushed past Violet on his way out of the room.

❊

Al could hardly wait for softball practice that night. He insisted on arriving early, which meant Millie had her pick of places from which to watch. Not that she would have had trouble finding a place to see. The regular crowd of spectators had dwindled over the past few practices. Now the only people who showed up to watch were the spouses and children of the players, along with the occasional friend like Violet. Even Thacker had not attended the last three, for which Al was grateful. He was not sure he could stomach seeing the man tonight. If he had not already arranged to take tomorrow off to extend his holiday weekend, he might even consider calling in sick. It wouldn't be a lie. If he had to face Thacker with the murdered camelias fresh in his memory, he *would* be sick.

Al retrieved the tote containing the team's balls and spare gloves from the trunk and slung the bag of bats over his shoulder while Millie spread her quilt in the place she'd selected.

"Look, there's Eulie and Norman." Millie nodded at an approaching truck as she set a basket in the center that included a picnic treat she'd prepared for the Wainright children. "I'm glad he's finally getting around."

When the Pilkington's pickup rolled to a stop, Little Norm got out and rounded the front bumper to help his father and mother down. Millie went to greet them while Al carried the equipment to the infield. He set the tote down and glanced around. After Saturday's practice, their softball field would once again become a pasture, home to the crankiest bull in three counties.

Parents settled, Little Norm joined Al on the field. Though itching to make his announcement, Al nevertheless greeted the Goose Creek pitcher with his customary reserve, scanning the arriving cars. Where was the mayor?

The Geddeses, Alice, Paul, and Fred had all arrived before Al finally spotted Jerry's car. Normally the first one there and bubbling enthusiasm, tonight the team's coach approached with a slow step, his feet dragging. Cindie, looking resolved but equally unenthusiastic, trod across the grass at his side.

When they approached the team Jerry lifted a hand to wave. "Hello, everyone. Sorry we're late." He glanced at those gathered around home plate. "Where are Justin and Susan?"

"They'll be here in a minute." Al couldn't hold in his news another second. "Before we start practice, I've got great news."

Everyone's attention fixed on him. From the sidelines, he caught Millie's grin and returned it.

"Oh?" Jerry arched an eyebrow. "What's that, Al?"

"We're going to win this game." He straightened, exuding confidence from his stance.

Several doubtful expressions appeared. Fred shoved his hands in his pockets and scuffed his shoe against the plastic base.

"I think we'll do okay," Sharon said. "We're a lot better than when we first started."

Alice nodded, her wide-set eyes guileless.

Paul, who had stepped up to the shortstop position when Junior broke his arm, squinted. "As long as they're not too good we might not embarrass ourselves."

"No, really." Al spread his grin around the circle and settled it on Jerry. "We're going to win. We have a new shortstop, and he's good."

The rumble of an approaching motorcycle sounded in the air. Jerry barely glanced over his shoulder, his gaze fixed intently on Al.

"We do? Who'd you find?"

Al lifted a hand and pointed. "Him."

They all turned as Justin, with Susan behind him, pulled his bike to a stop and lowered the kickstand. They climbed off and removed their helmets.

Jerry whipped back around, excitement flickering in his eyes. "You mean Justin?"

"That's right." Al's smile took on a measure of pride. "He's moving in with Millie and me. We've arranged for him to do some repair work for us in exchange for rent."

"He was willing to do that?" Paul asked. "Move here from Frankfort just so he could play on our team for one game?"

"Oh, I think he's got another reason for moving to Goose Creek," Cindie said, her gaze fixed on Justin, who was helping Susan out of her riding jacket.

"The lease on his apartment over in Frankfort is a month-to-month deal. He has to give a two week notice, but he said he'll go ahead and move this weekend to make it official."

When Al called Justin and presented the idea a couple of hours ago, he thought he'd have a tough job convincing him. Justin surprised him by agreeing immediately. Seemed he'd been considering a move to Goose Creek for some time.

A hopeful gleam flickered in the mayor's eyes. "With Justin at shortstop, we might pull this off after all."

Cindie marched across their circle and shoved her ball glove at Paul's chest. "You can have centerfield back. I quit."

Laughing, Jerry hugged her. "I did promise you wouldn't have to play if we found a replacement."

Their new shortstop and the town's veterinarian approached the field, and the team turned toward them, applauding. A blush stained Justin's cheeks, but Susan beamed. Apparently Justin's girlfriend wasn't opposed to having him live a bit closer.

Jerry clapped Justin on the back and drew him in to their circle. "Listen," he told the team, "let's keep this quiet. I want to watch Theo's face the first time he sees our team's star player in action."

As practice officially began, Al glanced toward Millie. Surrounded on her quilt by the tousle-haired Wainright children, she gave him a nod of approval. Al congratulated himself. He'd come up with a way to help the softball team *and* help his wife achieve her repair goals *and* save his retirement fund a few dollars, all at the same time. Brilliance, that's what it was. Sheer brilliance.

## Chapter Fourteen

Thomas pulled off the interstate on Friday afternoon and followed the curvy two-lane road toward Goose Creek. The air conditioner in the Lexus was working overtime to battle the combination of record-high temperatures and sunlight beating through the windshield. Only July first, and central Kentucky had already seen several days in the mid-nineties and humidity in the eighty-percent range. In spite of the cool air blowing on him, the collar of his golf shirt had stayed damp with sweat the whole way from Paducah.

Or maybe it wasn't the weather that made him damp under the collar. Three conversations awaited him in the little town where his daughter had settled. He was looking forward to only one of them.

Ahead on the right, he spied the spiraling old house where Susan's morning receptionist lived. Impressive, with all those peaks and that turret. The sprawling lawn appeared unkempt, though, desperately in need of attention. He slowed when he caught sight of a motorcycle parked on the cracked and broken pavement in the half-circle in front of the house. Hinkle's. And at the end of the driveway a utility truck. Thomas was aware of the handyman work he'd been employed to do there, but last night on the phone Susan surprised him with news of the man's intention to move to Goose Creek.

The more he considered the arrangement, the less surprised Thomas was. A transparent maneuver to get close to his daughter. The young man had ingratiated himself with Susan's receptionist and apparently a good portion of the town, judging by her account of the softball team's excitement at the news. And now he would be living less than three miles away.

Shrugging off the thought, Thomas slowed the car. Might as well get the first, and most distasteful, conversation over with immediately.

He turned onto the Richardsons' long driveway and parked his Lexus behind the motorcycle. Shiny and clean, he had to admit. Not a smudge on the paint nor a speck of dirt on the chrome. Turning toward the house, he scanned the multileveled roof. At that steep pitch, it must have been quite a job shingling that roof. And it looked immaculate. With grudging appreciation, he acknowledged that the job had been professionally accomplished.

Voices drifted to him from the backyard, so Thomas headed in that direction. The utility truck, from which hung ladders, extension cords and various tools, bore a magnetic sign on the door: *Hinkle the Handyman.*

When he rounded a pair of giant lilac bushes, Thomas spied the owner. Al, his name was. They'd met once or twice. The man stood in the shade of a tree, spraying the trunk with a hose. Though why he would water a huge tree like that, Thomas couldn't imagine. The thing was obviously healthy, with a dense leafy canopy that towered into the sky. Didn't the man know the roots on a tree this old were so far below ground that water from a hose would never reach them?

He wrinkled his nose. And what was that terrible odor?

A dog sleeping in a patch of sunlight caught sight of him and, barking, raced across the grass in his direction. Beagle mix, by the looks of it.

"Oh, hello." On the porch, Susan's morning receptionist straightened from her work at some task on a patio table.

"Hello." He stooped to rub the dog's head.

Al turned off the sprayer and tossed the hose on the ground. "Jeffries, right?" He approached, offering a hand.

"Thomas, please." He resisted the urge to dry his hand on his trousers.

Al laughed. "Sorry about that. Good day for yard work."

"Kind of hot," Thomas said.

From the porch, Millie asked, "Can I get you some iced tea or lemonade?"

"No. I'm here to see Hinkle." He glanced toward the house. "I saw his motorcycle out front. Is he here?"

Curiosity overtook the woman's features. "I'll go get him."

Al stopped her as she turned. "Millie, maybe Thomas would like to talk to Justin privately."

Thomas shot him a grateful look.

"Oh." Clearly disappointed, Millie returned to the table. "Go on in. He's in the parlor. Down the hallway to the left."

He entered the house through a pair of French doors, and as they closed behind him he heard her excited whisper: "What do you suppose he..."

Finding himself in a long dining room, he skirted an ornate table and exited on the other side. A voluminous entry hall rang with the pounding of a hammer. He paused a moment to gather his wits. He'd determined the necessity of this conversation a few days ago, and had been thinking about how it might go. A fresh sheen of sweat erupted on his neck, and he twitched at his collar to cool himself. Unpleasant though it might be, he'd best get it over with.

He rounded the corner and entered the parlor.

Hinkle stood with his back to the door holding a wooden frame against a piece of drywall with one hand and pounding a nail with the other. A fine sheen of dust covered his clothing and dark hair. With every strike of the hammer, a fresh puff of drywall dust danced into the air. An area rug had been rolled up and pushed to the side, and canvas drop cloths covered the furniture.

When the nail was sunk, Thomas scuffed his foot to produce a sound.

Hinkle turned. His eyes widened, then darkened with a wary concern. "Mr. Jeffries." He set the hammer down, his gaze remaining on Thomas's face, and snatched up a towel to wipe his hands. "I'm surprised to see you."

"I expect so." Thomas didn't intend to clip the words short. This conversation might prove more difficult than he'd anticipated.

"You want to sit down?" Hinkle lunged across the room and whipped the canvas off of a sofa.

Thomas waved aside the offer. "We won't be long. I came to ask your help with something."

The young man stopped in the act of folding the canvas. "Okay."

"I have a...friend who needs some work done. I'm helping her put together a business plan, and we need an estimate on the repairs. Would you be willing to give us a hand? It might lead to a job, if your estimate is reasonable."

The young man's eyes narrowed, and he thought for a moment before answering. "Is this job in Paducah?"

The reason for his caution became clear. He suspected Thomas of trying to lure him out of town and away from Susan. A logical conclusion, and not a bad idea if Thomas had thought of it a few months ago.

"No, it's here. In Goose Creek. The work is to be done on a building on Main Street, where my friend is opening her establishment."

"Oh." Clearly confused, and still more than a little cautious, Hinkle gave a slow nod. "Sure. I'll be happy to do that for you."

"Fine." Thomas nodded and extracted a folded paper from his pocket. "I have a list of the necessary repairs." He shifted his weight. Now came the difficult part of the conversation. "I want to talk to you about something else as well. Susan."

Now the boy's suspicion came to the fore. His expression closed over, stubbornness easily seen in his rigid stance. "Go ahead."

"She tells me she's grown"—he cleared his throat—"quite fond of you."

"I'm quite fond of her too."

"Yes, well, you should understand something about Susan." The words of his rehearsed speech rolled off his tongue. "I know my opinion is biased, but I think she's highly intelligent and hardworking, and she has an innate desire to achieve that will enable her to succeed at whatever she dedicates herself to."

The corners of Hinkle's mouth twitched the slightest bit. "She's also compassionate and understanding and beautiful."

"Those too." At least they agreed on Susan's virtues. "On the other hand, she's easily distracted, not very organized, and lacks experience."

Now he did smile. "That's part of her charm."

"Plus, she's dismal at managing her finances."

"She doesn't need to, does she?" Hinkle dipped his head forward. "She has you for that."

Unable to bear looking into the face of the man who had stolen his daughter from him, Thomas paced to the bay window. He clasped his hands behind his back, staring outside with unseeing eyes. Time to stop thinking in those terms. He spoke the words he'd dreaded for days.

"That has become a problem. As long as she has me directing her, she won't develop those skills."

In the long silence that followed, Thomas fought the urge to turn around and see Hinkle's face.

"Are you saying you've changed your mind about moving to Goose Creek?" he finally asked.

"I have. I think it's in my daughter's best interest if I stay where I am. Not that I will pull my support," he hurried to say. Let there be no mistake about that. "I'll be available whenever she needs me. Just..." He filled his lungs with a slow breath. "From a distance."

No sound from behind for so long that Thomas finally did glance over his shoulder. Hinkle stood stock-still, confusion still clear on his face. Confusion and something else. A flicker of understanding, perhaps.

"I'm sure that wasn't an easy decision," he finally said.

"It was not." Thomas struggled to keep his tone even. "And the only reason I feel comfortable making it is..." His throat went dry. "Because of you."

"Me?"

Nodding, Thomas turned to face the young man. "I've conducted some discreet research into your business." Hinkle's eyebrows arched. Thomas straightened his spine, unashamed. What decent father wouldn't use every available resource to protect his daughter's welfare? "Your business plan is solid, your financial structure stable. Your references are admirable. On paper you exhibit many of the qualities Susan lacks."

Hinkle shook his head. "I don't understand. What are you saying?"

"That you can help her in the areas where she needs help. Where she lacks experience, you can support her. Help her grow. And perhaps she has qualities that will benefit you as well. In other words, your skills complement each other's."

Silence stretched between them. The young man's eyes unfocused as he processed the information Thomas had given him.

"Nobody will ever take your place in Susan's life," he finally said, his voice soft.

Thomas lifted his nose in the air. "Of course not. She'll always be my little girl." Then he ducked his head. "But maybe it's time she learned how to be an adult."

Another long silence, and finally Hinkle nodded. "I understand. In that case, sir, there's something I'd like to talk to *you* about." He gestured toward the sofa. "You might want to sit down for this."

Thomas recognized the look on Hinkle's face, though he had not seen it in quite a while and never in the current context. A dreaded sense of the inevitable settled over him, and he took a seat.

※

Thomas looked forward to his next conversation with far more enthusiasm. He parked the Lexus at the curb in front of Tuesday's house and, picking up a folder from the passenger seat, approached the porch. The front door opened as his foot touched the step.

Tuesday beamed at him. "I wondered if you were going to call and cancel today. Our appointment was for half an hour ago."

The door swung wide and she invited him inside with a gesture. Today she looked even more bohemian than usual, with purple toenails, a pair of jeans cropped at the calf, and a loose-fitting tunic that looked as if a flower show had exploded in her vicinity. She had made an effort to tame her wild curls by twisting them into a pair of braids that swung halfway down her arms.

"My last appointment took longer than anticipated," he explained as she shut the door behind him. "Am I too late for a massage? Do you have another appointment after mine?"

Her eyes rolled expansively. "Puh-leease. You're the only one who's been on my bed since I moved to town."

He hid a wince. If she wanted to succeed in a conservative town like Goose Creek, she really needed to take care in selecting her words. They'd work on that later.

"That's about to change." He extended the folder. "Here's your business plan. There are still a few holes, such as the cost of building repairs, but that's coming."

"Ooh, this is so exciting."

Taking the folder, she planted herself on the sofa, her legs contorted into a pretzel-like arrangement at which Thomas could only marvel. There may have been a time when his limbs moved like that, but he couldn't remember. A tickle of anticipation erupted as he watched her open the folder, reminiscent of the feeling he experienced when Susan came down the stairs on Christmas morning for her first glimpse of the gifts piled beneath the tree.

Tuesday looked up, eyes round and sparkling. "This is an amazing idea. Why didn't I think of it?"

Unable to suppress a grin, he shrugged. "Sometimes it takes a second pair of eyes. And in this case, a thorough investigation of the customer base."

She flipped over a page, and then another. "I could never have put together something like this." Gratitude shone in the gaze she lifted to him. "You really are good at this stuff, Thomas."

He accepted the compliment with a nod. "And you're talented at what you do. As you said last week, we make a good team. And I took the liberty of showing your plan to a couple of my coworkers at the bank. They agreed that this is a financial investment they'd be comfortable approving. So before you make a decision on a lender, we'll do some comparison shopping."

With a loud squeal she launched herself off the cushion and flew across the room. Thomas was nearly bowled over when she threw her arms around him and hugged with surprising strength.

"Oh. Sorry." She stepped back and tugged the hem of her tunic to straighten it. "No hanky-panky between business partners. Now, you go on in there and strip down, and I'll work you over like you've never seen, baby!"

Shaking his head, Thomas headed down the hall. They *really* needed to focus on her conversation skills.

❋

Ninety minutes later he pulled the Lexus into the parking lot of the Goose Creek Animal Clinic and sat for a moment with his hands on the steering wheel. Now came the final conversation of the day, the one that would prove to be the most emotional. More difficult even than talking to Hinkle. Thomas did not enjoy the taste of crow, and he was about to fill his plate with a large helping.

Inside he found the waiting room empty and the afternoon receptionist clearing her desk.

She fixed a hesitant smile on him. "Hello, Mr. Jeffries."

An improvement, since the first few times he'd encountered the woman she had been too shy to speak. Perhaps she was gaining confidence.

"Good afternoon. Alice, is it?"

The smile blossomed. "That's right. Your daughter is in exam room one with the last patient of the day. Did you want me to print off the weekly accounting report so you can look it over while you wait?"

Though that was the task he typically performed when he arrived, today's visit was anything but typical. He shook his head. "No, thank you. I'll wait in her office." He took a step in that direction, and then stopped. "Um, have a nice holiday weekend, Alice."

"You too, Mr. Jeffries. Will you be at the ballgame on Monday?"

"Oh yes. Most certainly." That was one game he could not afford to miss.

"I'll see you then."

The small confines of the clinic office were not conducive to pacing, but he managed to stride from the wall to the door several times before Susan entered.

She crossed the distance to give him a quick hug. "Alice said you were waiting. Why are you here so early on a Friday night?" Her eyes widened. "Did you come up here to start your new job in Lexington?"

"No, but that's what I want to talk to you about."

Instead of seating her in the rolling office chair, he gestured for her to take one of the plastic chairs in front of the desk and then squeezed into the second. During this conversation he wanted nothing between them, even a desk.

She looked surprised but sat where he indicated. Creases appeared on her brow. "Is everything okay?" Her hands gripped the arms of her chair. "You didn't quit your job, did you?"

"No, and I don't intend to."

"I don't understand."

He clasped his hands and rested them in his lap. He'd rehearsed this speech too, but in the face of Susan's questioning gaze, the words lodged in his throat. Parenting was never this hard when she was a girl, or even a teenager.

"I've decided not to move to Goose Creek."

Her eyes moved as she studied his face. "The bank wouldn't let you transfer to Lexington, would they?"

"No, they wouldn't. They were more than willing to make me the regional manager over central Kentucky, but that is several levels below my position as an officer."

"So you decided to stay on as a vice president."

"I accepted the manager's job." He flashed a brief smile. "For exactly eighteen hours. Then I withdrew my request and the president graciously ripped up my acceptance letter."

"It must have been a pretty big pay cut, huh?"

"Yes, but that wasn't the issue. You were." Questions sprang into her eyes, but he continued before she could speak. "Susan, when your mother died I felt..." He swallowed. "So alone. All I had was you. And all you had was me. I made a vow to never let you suffer the loneliness I suffered. That I would be there for you always."

She leaned forward and covered his hands with hers. "You have been, Daddy. No one could ask for a better father than you."

"I wish that were true, but I've come to realize that I've protected you too closely. I haven't let you learn the things a person can only learn by doing them alone. And especially by failing and suffering the consequences."

"If you mean this clinic"—she gestured to indicate the building around them—"then you can't let me fail or you'll lose your investment."

He shook his head. "I have every confidence in your abilities to make this business succeed. I'm talking about relationships." He drew in a breath. "Susan, I'm afraid you're too dependent on me." His chest heaved with a rueful laugh. "And I'm definitely too dependent on you. It's time we both expanded our horizons, and we can't do that if we're living under the same roof."

"This is about Justin, isn't it?" Her lips trembled while her gaze locked on to his. "Have you decided you approve of him after all?"

"Let's just say I've decided to trust your judgment where Justin is concerned." There. He'd said the boy's name, and it didn't kill him.

She sprang forward and threw her arms around his neck. "Thank you, Daddy. You really are the *best* father in the world."

Thomas reveled in the compliment not because it was true, but because his daughter *thought* it was true. He squeezed her tight, and when she returned to her chair he nearly wept at the emptiness of his arms. Half of his heart had just been ripped out and launched aloft. He had no doubt it would sprout wings and fly—directly into the arms of someone else.

But that was where it should be.

In the empty place in his chest a sense of rightness seeped in, swelling like water rising slowly in a well. His little girl would succeed. Of that he had no doubt.

"Well." He slapped his hands on his knees and pushed off of the chair. "I need to get back to Lexington. I have some shopping to do."

She stood too. "Shopping? For what?"

"Shoes." He extended a foot. "I think my feet are growing. Mine have recently become too tight."

# Chapter Fifteen

Ah, Saturday. Still wearing his pajamas, Al took his coffee to the verandah (He actually thought the word. Millie must be rubbing off on him.) and stood at the railing, gazing at the pond across a small but satisfying stretch of lush, green grass. No weeds marred the area on which he'd focused for the last month. Now that he'd achieved the perfect balance of fertilizer and weed killer, he would expand his area of focus. The front lawn would have to wait until later. A man could only do so much, after all. But before summer's end not a single weed would be visible from the vantage point of the gazebo.

No weeds, but plenty of squirrels.

They scampered across the yard now, darting between the shepherd's crooks in an attempt to scrounge any seed they might have missed. The bird feeders remained empty. Why bother, when they'd be empty again within hours and his yard filled with plump, satisfied rodents?

The door behind him opened and Millie came to his side, holding the coffee carafe. She drew in a deep breath. "It smells so much better out here."

He agreed. "I guess washing the tree trunks diluted the wildcat urine enough. I wasn't sure it would work."

"Thank goodness." She refilled his coffee mug. "What do you have planned for today?"

"Yard work."

"Again?" She squinted at his forehead, which had begun to peel.

"This yard is a career in itself," he informed her. "Besides, I have a new plan."

Doubt stole over her features. "Not more squirrel repellent, I hope."

"Not this time. I've decided on a new approach." He sipped coffee. It needed more honey. "Want to go to Home Depot with me? They're having a Fourth of July sale."

She shook her head. "I can't. Violet and I are going over to Cindie's to iron letters on the softball team's T-shirts."

Ah, the anticipated T-shirt. "Then maybe I'll have a surprise waiting when you get home."

"I'm sure we'll be there most of the day. I'll catch up with you at the practice." She rose on her tiptoes to kiss his cheek. "Breakfast will be ready in ten minutes. And don't forget to put on sunscreen."

"Yes, dear."

He lingered after she left, contemplating the area before him. If this approach didn't work, he'd throw in the towel.

❉

The last team practice progressed better than Jerry had dared to hope. The hot July sun beating down unmercifully kept most of the spectators away, which suited him fine. Only a handful of people lined the other side of the fence. Seated in the shade of a beach umbrella, Norman with his bandaged foot and a crutch propped against his chair and Junior with his arm in a sling looked like battle casualties in a hospital ward.

After they'd been working for an hour, Cindie's car pulled onto the gravel driveway. Jerry called the team in.

"That's enough for today, everyone," he shouted as they made their way to home plate. "No sense exhausting ourselves in this heat any more than necessary."

"How do you think we'll do on Monday?" Sharon asked as she accepted an icy bottle of water from Al.

"I think we look great." Justin twisted off the top of his water, gulped half of it down, and poured the rest over his head.

"We'll do just fine." Jerry waved Cindie over. "We've got a T-shirt for everyone. Some of the ladies have been working to get them ready today."

Cindie arrived with a stack of maroon shirts draped over her arm. "Some of them might be a little crooked, but I think they turned out well." She examined the tag on the top one and handed it to Fred.

He held it up for the team's inspection. White letters spelling out *Goose Creek* arched over a silhouette of a bird in flight. Privately, Jerry thought the bird looked more like a buzzard than a goose, but the icon had been sketched by Fred's wife, Wilma, so he kept his opinion to himself.

Al received his shirt and held it up in front of him. "Mine's too big."

"Blame your wife," Cindie said. "Millie chose that one for you."

He glanced toward the onlookers. "Where is Millie?"

"Oh, she took my kids to help with an errand." Alice held her shirt up to her shoulders to test the fit. "I think they might be getting ice cream."

When the shirts had been distributed and everyone exclaimed over Wilma's design and the ladies' efforts, Jerry lifted a hand to get their attention.

"I want to thank you all for your hard work over the last month. I know some of you weren't enthusiastic about playing." He glanced at Dr. Susan, who grinned at Justin. "But you did, and I appreciate it."

Little Norm piped up. "We appreciate you too, Mayor. You and Justin have whipped us into shape."

A smattering of applause indicated everyone's agreement, and Jerry ducked his head. "Thanks. Some of you know at times I've been a little uptight about this game." He glanced at Al. "But even if we

don't win, I'm proud of what we've done together. You guys are great."
He looked at Justin. "Any final advice from our assistant coach?"

"Just relax and have fun." Justin projected confidence with a smile
around the circle. "We'll do fine."

Jerry nodded. "All right then. Let's all go home and get rested up
for Monday. I'll see you at the ballpark at nine thirty." They started
to move away. "Oh, and don't forget the water tower unveiling that
afternoon."

"That's right." Little Norm's chest swelled to twice its normal size.
"It's gonna be awesome."

They sauntered toward the opening in the fence, though Cindie
lagged behind. "Good speech," she told him.

"Thanks." He bent down and pried home plate out of the ground.
Glancing to be sure no one was close enough to hear, he added,
"Would it be wrong to say a prayer in church tomorrow that we beat
the pants off of Theo's team?"

She grinned. "I've always thought of God as a Creeker."

❋

Since the practice was shortened, Al showered and changed before
Millie arrived home. Reclining in a chair in the shade of the verandah with a glass of iced tea, he watched her get out of the car, her gaze
fixed on his handiwork.

"Albert!" Purse slung over her shoulder, she came toward him with
wide eyes. "I must say, I never thought I'd see the day."

"You know what Violet would say." He lifted a hand in a gesture of
defeat. "If you can't beat 'em, join 'em."

Gone were the useless traps, stored in the attic until he could figure out what to do with them. He'd removed the shepherd's hooks
from the middle of the lawn, leaving the manicured stretch of grass
empty and spacious. On the other side of the gazebo a modest four
of them stood in a line, the feeders full and well attended by a cluster of wrens. From the eaves of the gazebo hung three planters. Deep

pink, brilliant yellow, and dazzling purple blossoms overflowed in a rainbow of beauty.

But what had drawn Millie's attention, as he knew they would, were the squirrel feeders.

He'd mounted one to the trunk of each of the huge shade trees and filled them with a blend of corn, peanuts, and sunflower seeds specially designed for squirrels. In the past fifteen minutes, he'd identified six distinct individuals among the herd that crowded the yard.

"I'm stunned." She stepped onto the verandah and stooped to rub Rufus's ears. "Absolutely stunned."

"My theory is if I feed them something they like, they'll leave the bird food alone." He gestured with his tea glass to the feeders. "So far it seems to be working."

Tossing her purse on the table, she slid onto the cushioned lawn chair beside his, Rufus settling on the porch between them. "Look. There's a cardinal."

Al nodded as a bright red bird winged to a landing on one of the feeders, scattering several of the wrens into flight. "He's been here a couple of times, and his mate once. And a hummingbird has already found the flowers. I think I'll pick up one of those nectar feeders next week."

Millie giggled. "Goodness, look at them squabble."

Al followed her gaze. Two squirrels had apparently selected the same feeder, and neither was inclined to share. "See the one with the fuller tail? I think he's the leader. I've been watching him boss the rest of them around."

"Oh, look at the little one. It must be a baby."

"Here goes the brave one again." He pointed out a squirrel that had leaped out of the tree and was making his way across the yard, stopping every few feet to rise up and inspect the area. "Watch this."

The animal headed for the only squirrel feeder that was not attached to a tree. Al had set one of the garden hooks on the opposite side of the yard from the birds' area and hung a wooden feeder with a short length of chain. As they watched, the rodent he'd come to think of as Gutsy arrived at the base of the hook. With no visible effort, he launched himself forward and grabbed the rod two feet off the ground.

"It isn't greased?" Millie asked.

"What's the point? They'd only drop from the branch above it."

Gutsy scampered upward, halting at a point parallel to the feeder. With a hop he crossed the eight-inch distance and landed on the plastic ledge. The feeder began to spin, Gutsy clinging to the side like a child on a wound-up tire swing, tail twitching.

Millie clapped her hands to her mouth, delighted laughter bubbling from her. "That is hysterical!"

Grinning at the creature's antics, Al nodded. "Several of them have attempted, but he's the only one who keeps coming back. I think he enjoys the ride."

A movement to the right drew their attention. The Boss leaped from the feeder he'd monopolized and darted across the grass.

Al sat upright in his chair "Where does he think he's going?"

The plucky little fellow paused beside the gazebo, cocked his head toward his audience on the verandah, and then darted toward the bird feeders.

"No!" Al shouted, fluttering his hand in the air in that direction. "You stay away from there."

Birds scattered and disappeared as the Boss scurried up the ungreased pole.

Utterly defeated, Al sank back in his chair. So much for his last-ditch effort to enjoy the birds. "I give up."

Millie opened her mouth to say something, but stopped when Rufus perked to attention. The dog launched himself off the gazebo's deck, barking with fury, and flew toward the offending squirrel. As Al's jaw dropped, the beagle executed a flying leap toward the feeder. He fell several feet short, of course, but succeeded in startling the Boss. The squirrel flung himself off the feeder and executed a hasty escape toward the nearest tree trunk.

Mission accomplished, Rufus trotted back to them with his head held high.

"Good dog." Millie swung her feet around and bent to give Rufus an enthusiastic ear rub.

"What happened to snap him out of his funk?"

She beamed up at Al. "I think he's finally starting to feel at home here."

When Millie finished her praise, Rufus approached Al's chair with an expectant air.

Al obliged. "Good job." He scrubbed the place where Rufus's tail met his back and the dog's eyes closed with pleasure. "Maybe you're not completely worthless after all."

# Chapter Sixteen

On Independence Day Al beat the sun up by several hours. Careful not to wake Millie, he grabbed his slippers and crept out of their bedroom. He tiptoed through the entry hall, mindful that sound magnified as it rose up the huge stairway and not wanting to disturb Justin. To his right lay the formal living room, a space he considered superfluous and Millie adored. He ignored that and instead entered the room on the left.

A peaceful charm imbued the parlor. Passing through the generous wooden doorframe, he sometimes felt as though he'd stepped back to a gentler time. The crystals dangling from the opulent chandelier tinkled gently in a nearly imperceptible breeze from the air conditioner. He glanced toward the magnificent mantel—at the moment barely visible in the darkness—that had been hand-carved before the turn of the last century. Slippers scuffing on the hardwood floor, he crossed to the outrageously expensive bay window and settled himself on the cushioned window seat.

Outside, the moon cast a white light on the front lawn, unbroken by artificial glare. Even in daylight, no houses were visible from this view, their images obscured by the trees and a gentle swell in the land this side of the road. He liked that about this location. Solitude.

That was one thing this house offered that the one on Mulberry Avenue hadn't, crowded as it was on all sides by neighbors.

The air conditioner ceased, and silence deepened around him. It was almost as though the house itself slept, and he was the only one awake in the world.

Never had he pictured himself and Millie in a place like this. If he'd considered their waning days at all, it had been with the assumption that they would live out their lives in the house they'd built together, where their children had grown up. They'd travel, enjoy visiting new places. Spoil their grandchildren together. Mostly he'd focused his efforts on the financial aspect of their retirement. Perhaps a little too much focus?

He leaned his head sideways against the window, soaking in the coolness the glass had gathered during the night. One thing had not changed in almost forty years. He loved the woman sleeping upstairs. At times she drove him crazy, but he loved her. More than money. More than a house. As long as they were together, what did it matter where they lived?

❋

"Happy Fourth of July!"

Al hefted the tote out of his trunk and returned the mayor's greeting. "You too. Give me a hand with these bats, would you?"

Jerry slung the bag over his shoulder and together they headed for the baseball field. The mayors had agreed on a neutral location, the field behind the high school in the next county over. Judging by the number of cars already occupying parking spaces, the distance was no deterrent to attendance.

"There's Fred." With a nod Al indicated a car pulling off of the street.

"I think I saw the Geddes's car parked over there. Yeah, there they are." Jerry waved to catch the couple's attention.

By the time they reached the rear of the parking lot, almost the entire team had arrived. Justin and Susan roared up, and the group gathered around the motorcycle as the two peeled off their jackets.

Raking a hand through his hair, Justin grinned at them. "Hey, we look pretty good. Like a real team."

Al did not disagree, though he'd grumbled at the image in the bathroom mirror before he left the house. The shoulders on this gigantic T-shirt hung halfway down his arms, and the hem was so long he'd had to bunch it up to tuck it in his pants. Millie defended her selection of this size by saying the only extras they had after outfitting the players were small or XXL. As he'd feared, he looked like a pudgy old man.

But the others looked good. And eager. Alice practically bounced as they walked toward the field, her step light. Chuck joked with Paul while they carried a cooler full of bottled water between them, and Little Norm bragged to Sharon that he was planning to pitch a no-hitter. Even Susan didn't drag her feet, though she did keep smoothing her hair behind her ear with a jerky motion and casting nervous glances at Justin.

The metal bleachers on both sides already held a smattering of spectators, and more people filed into them as the team approached. From the top row, Woody Edwards stood and cupped his hands around his mouth. "Good luck, Creekers!"

Jerry waved, and then the smile faded. "Here comes Theo."

The team came to a halt as the mayor of Morleyville approached wearing a bright yellow shirt and a politician's smile.

"Finally showed up, did you? We've been here for an hour already." He gestured behind him, where a group of similarly clad people had claimed the Home Team dugout.

"Eager to meet your fate, are you?" Jerry hefted the bag higher on his shoulder.

"Looking forward to cooking us some goose for our holiday dinner." Theo's molars came into view. "Just kidding. We're all here to have fun, aren't we?"

Al found himself disliking the man. No wonder Jerry wanted so badly to beat him.

"You bet we are." Jerry glanced at the Goose Creek team. "Right?"

"Yeah!"

"You know it."

"Reckon so." Little Norm pounded a fist into his glove and managed to look twice his normal size.

Not intimidated, the Morleyville mayor nodded. "Fine, just fine." His gaze returned to Jerry. "You sure you don't want to place a little wager on your team?"

Jerry maintained his smile. "That would take the fun out of it."

"Whatever you say." Theo clapped him on the back, which Jerry endured with more aplomb than Al could have managed. "Good game, y'all."

He sauntered away with a step that could only be described as a swagger.

"Is he always like that?" Justin asked, his gaze fixed on the man's back.

Jerry nodded. "Always."

"How come they get to be the home team?" Little Norm asked.

"Because I lost the toss." Jerry turned his back on his nemesis. "Doesn't matter. The dugouts are the same. Come on, let's put our stuff in there and warm up."

The team moved toward the Visitor dugout. Al deposited his tote on the dirt and scanned the rapidly filling bleachers. Millie had better hurry or she wouldn't get a seat. She'd left the house before him to pick up the Wainright children so Alice could be on time.

"Bert! Over here!"

Heaving a longsuffering sigh, Al located Thacker near the fence, his hand waving wildly above his head. Of course he would be here. Since he had not showed up for practices, Al had held out hope that he wouldn't attend today. No such luck. And worse, he held a stapled stack of papers. As Al approached the chain link fence he spied a familiar-looking chart on top.

"I tried to get the mayor's attention, but he's busy coaching." Thacker thrust the papers toward Al. "I've got some data that will help the team."

"Weren't you paying attention when we met in the mayor's office?" Al shook his head. "The guys don't want to see your analysis."

"This is different. Just take a look." He turned his head. "Oh, there's Lulu about to drop our hot dogs." He shouted, "Coming, sugar buns!" and hurried away.

Al glanced at the papers. How could the man say this was different? The chart looked the same as the last one. The title read *Team Skills Analysis* above a line graph with dozens of data points. Some people just didn't understand the word *no*.

Setting the report on the bench in the dugout, he went about laying out the team's bats.

❈

The game kicked off with a whistle from one of the fresh-faced teenagers they'd hired to umpire. Jerry stood at the entrance of the dugout and watched as the first batter, Sharon, popped a foul that was caught by the Morleyville catcher. Fred came next and hit a solid line drive. It was scooped by the second baseman and lobbed to first in plenty of time to stomp on the base.

"Sorry," Fred muttered as he passed on his way into the dugout.

"Don't worry about it." Justin slapped him on the shoulder and then clapped and called, "Come on, Suz. Knock it out of the park."

Susan approached the batter's box like she was going to a funeral. From where Jerry stood, he could see the bat trembling. As she took her stance, he formed an unspoken prayer that she wouldn't throw up. Three perfectly good balls whizzed past her. The first two she didn't even swing at. He couldn't be sure, but her eyes might have been closed. She swung at the third, but missed.

"Strike three!" The umpire's call was met with a cheer from the Morleyville supporters and a groan from the bleachers behind Jerry.

"Don't worry about it." He clapped his hands as she shuffled by. "There's a lot of game left."

A very long game, he feared.

Morleyville headed for their dugout and his team filed onto the field. Jerry ducked into the dugout to grab his glove, nodding at Norman and Junior, who had been given shirts and invited to sit with the team. Cindie's idea, which Jerry appreciated even more today. At least their bench wouldn't be empty when Goose Creek took the field.

When he turned, he almost groaned. Theo stood near first base and apparently intended to coach his team from there.

"Hope you've got some heavy hitters further down your lineup." He delivered the comment with one of his annoying grins. "Otherwise this is gonna be the shortest game in history."

Since he couldn't think of a comeback worthy of his office, Jerry marched past him without speaking. He planted himself a few feet beyond first base.

The first batter up for Morleyville was a woman.

"That's my niece. She's home from college for the summer. Got a volleyball scholarship." Theo's voice held a gloating tone. "She's quite the athlete."

Terrific.

Little Norm tossed the ball up and down a few times while the batter adjusted her feet and hefted her bat. His head turned as he glanced around the infield. With a nod at Fred, he threw a pitch. The bat hesitated, swung, and connected. A low, fast hit toward the unmanned spot in left-center. In one smooth motion Justin charged in that direction, scooped it off the ground, and threw it directly into Jerry's waiting glove. Jerry stepped on the plate seconds before the runner. Cheers erupted from the Goose Creek bleacher.

For the first time, Theo's expression lost some of its smugness. "I don't think I've seen that fellow before."

Jerry threw the ball to Little Norm. "That's Justin Hinkle, our newest resident. Just moved to town a few days ago, in fact." He couldn't help adding a taunt. "He's quite the athlete, isn't he?"

Theo's eyes narrowed. "You aren't trying to pull a fast one on me, are you, Selbo?"

"Who, me?"

With a wide-eyed smile, he returned to his position. That, at least, had been satisfying. Now, if only they could manage to score a run or two.

※

By the time Millie arrived with the children, the ballgame had begun. Yellow-shirted players were positioned around the field, and more were seated in the deep shadow of the Home Team's dugout. Oh dear. Morleyville had twice as many players as Goose Creek. If one of theirs got tired, there were a bunch of fresh replacements.

She scanned the bleachers and caught sight of Violet, seated alone. Millie led her little troop in that direction.

"How long have they been playing?" she asked as she settled the children.

"It's only the second inning."

Forest stood, head moving as he scanned the field. "How's my mom playing?"

"She's the belle of the ball," Violet answered.

A puzzled expression settled on the boy's face. "Huh?"

Millie interpreted. "That means she's the best."

"She caught two outs in the first inning and one in the second. And she got all the way to second base a few minutes ago before they caught her."

"Go Mama!" Fern shouted, and little Tansy bounced like a ball on her bench.

"What's the score?" Millie opened her bag and passed out the juice boxes she'd brought for the youngsters.

Violet cringed. "Four to nothing."

"Oh, dear."

Millie's gaze settled on Albert, who stood beside the row of bats he'd laid out on the ground. He looked quite official, if a little frumpy in that oversized shirt. As if aware of her regard, he turned to search the bleachers. She waved, and when he caught sight of her, he lifted a hand in a subtle acknowledgment.

"Hey, Mrs. R." Franklin Thacker, seated at the end of the bench behind her, called a question. "Did you get everything taken care of?"

With a smile at Lulu, she nodded. "Thank you for your help, Franklin."

"No prob-*lay*-mo. Let us know how it turns out." His gaze settled on Violet. "How's it shaking, Plum?"

Violet lifted her nose in the air, her expression frosty, and turned her attention to the field.

Millie patted her arm. Though friendly and at times even helpful, the man really was quite annoying.

※

As the game stretched on, Al's confidence flagged. From the downcast looks on the faces of the Goose Creek team, he wasn't the only one who feared the outcome of this game.

"What's the score now?" Seated in the dugout while the team fielded the bottom of the eighth inning, Junior scrubbed sweat from back of his neck with a dingy handkerchief.

Beside him on the bench, Norman aimed a scowl in his direction. "Ain't been no runs since the last time you asked. How's come you keep askin' the same dadburned question?"

"It's so hot my brain ain't a-workin' right." The younger man turned away from him and repeated his question to Al. "So what's the score?"

"Eight to four." Though there was no need for clarification, Al couldn't help adding, "Morleyville's in the lead."

"We 'uns could still get 'er done if'n we'd stop fiddlin' around and play ball." Norman slumped in the back corner of the dugout, where he'd insisted on sitting so his foot would be out of harm's way.

He'd brought his own stool from home on which to prop his injured appendage. "If'n I was out there, I could show 'em a thing or two."

In the bottom of the eighth inning, and with Morleyville's best hitters coming up to bat? Al didn't want to be the voice of gloom, but from where he sat their chances looked pretty dim.

"Bert! Come here a minute."

Al caught sight of Thacker at the entrance of the dugout, his arms dangling over the chain link fence. As if things weren't dismal enough. Heaving himself off the bench, Al left the scant shade of the dugout and entered the blistering sun to approach Thacker.

"Why isn't the mayor using the info I gave him?"

"This isn't the time, Franklin." Al faced the game, leaning on the fence beside his coworker. "In case you haven't noticed, things aren't going well."

An accusing frown settled on the man's features. "You haven't showed him my analysis, have you? Have you even looked at it yourself?"

"There hasn't been time." The excuse fell lamely from Al's lips. No, wait. Why make excuses? Thacker needed to face the truth, harsh though it may be. Apparently telling him once wasn't enough. "Listen, Franklin, we told you weeks ago that several people on the team were insulted by your analysis. If we start pulling out your reports and pinpointing their weaknesses now, they may take your head off."

Thacker's lower lip protruded, reminding Al of his boys when they were young. "If you'd read my report you'd know it isn't about our team."

That stopped Al. He peered at the man. "I glanced at that chart. It's a skill analysis, same as I saw before."

"But not our team's skills." He jerked his head across the field. "Theirs."

Al looked at the opposing dugout, the bench full of yellow-shirted players. Two stood on the sidelines, swinging bats and preparing to take their turns in the batter's box. "You analyzed their team?"

"Duh. Did I stutter?" Thacker rolled his eyes. "How could I run our team's data? In case you haven't noticed, I haven't watched a practice in weeks."

"I know, but I thought you'd changed your mind about your program after our meeting in Jerry's office."

Thacker planted his hands on his hips. "I told you then I would come up with a way to help. So I became a spy. I snuck into the enemy's camp." He cocked his head, lips screwed up in a twisted line. "Well, I didn't have to sneak. I just started going to their practices, watching and taking notes. They had a lot more people there to cheer them on, so nobody asked who I was or what I was doing there."

A grudging admiration blossomed in Al. Thacker hadn't given up when his first attempt to help was slapped down. Instead, he persisted. Even if the analysis turned out to be junk, his perseverance was impressive.

But if it helped...

"Are you saying your program came up with something that could help us?"

"Of course it did." He rested an arm across the top of the fence. "I might not be good at diplomacy, Bert, but I'm a really good programmer."

"Hold on a minute." Al dashed into the dugout and snatched the stapled papers off the bench. Returning, he flipped the top chart over. "Show me how to read this."

Thacker took the report, shuffled a few pages, and then presented it back to him. "That guy who's coming up to bat next? He's kind of a hot shot on their team."

Al glanced at the player in question. "He's scored a couple of times already."

"That's because Little Norm is throwing exactly the kind of pitch he likes. High, fast, and center. But look here." He tapped on the paper. "Every time he hits a slow, low one, he pops it to left field. *Every* time."

They exchanged a loaded glance. Hope flickered in the gloom that had overtaken Al's mood. He raced into the open, waving the report over his head to catch the umpire's attention.

"Time out!"

# Chapter Seventeen

Jerry dismissed his team and returned to his position near first base. As they jogged back to their places, he glanced back at Al. Beside him, Thacker continued to talk, tongue wagging a mile a minute while he thumped his report. Al's gaze connected with Jerry's, and he shrugged. If this worked, they might actually have a chance.

"What was that all about?" Theo's head swiveled from the Visitor dugout to Jerry. "Y'all looked pretty serious over there."

"Team secret," Jerry said, and then added with a secretive grin, "Just Goose talk."

Though it was impossible to cross his fingers inside a baseball glove, Jerry performed the gesture with the other hand. He caught Cindie's eye in the stands, and she splayed both hands in a clear question. He smiled in response.

The Goose Creek team in place, the Morleyville hitter approached the batter's box.

"This young man's been a great addition to our team." Thumbs hooked in his pockets, Theo's chest expanded. "Great ball player. A real inspiration."

Jerry ignored him.

The batter propped the bat between his shoes, stooped, and gathered a handful of dirt. Rubbing his hands together, a cloud of dust rose and then settled at his feet. He dusted his hands on his pants and grasped the handle of the bat.

Little Norm planted his feet and juggled the ball a few times. He bent his knees. Glanced over his shoulder. Jerry gave him a nod. Glanced the other way. Justin lifted a thumb. Chuck pounded a fist in his glove. Alice crouched, glove held at the ready.

Facing forward, Little Norm reared his arm back and let go with an underhanded pitch.

The moment the ball left the pitcher's hand, Justin raced backward into the field.

The ball arced, slow and sure, and descended toward the batter's box. Taking a step, the hitter swung. The bat connected with a *whack!* that echoed across the field. A solid hit.

The Morleyville crowd roared their approval as the ball soared through the air. On the ground, Justin darted sideways, head craned back, eyes on the ball.

And snagged it out of the air on the descent.

Now it was the Goose Creek crowd on their feet, clapping and cheering as the maroon-clad team jogged toward the dugout. Paul leaped and high-fived Chuck, both grinning like fiends.

Jerry turned to find Theo's narrow-eyed stare fixed on him.

"Not bad."

"I'd say that was pretty good for a cooked goose."

Jerry strutted past him to join his team in the dugout.

❈

Susan couldn't sit still. She paced to the wood railing that lined the dugout and hung on to the support post. If anyone had told her she would be so caught up in something as silly as a ballgame, she wouldn't have believed them. If they'd said she would actually bite her nails watching, she would have said they were nuts. And if they'd said she would cheer like a crazed fan, she would have called for a padded truck.

"Come on, Little Norm!" She took her fingernail from between her teeth long enough to clap encouragement.

Standing in the sunlight next to Al, Justin turned an amused grin her way.

The Goose Creek team had made the most of their last time at bat. News of Franklin's inside information acted like a shot of adrenaline and launched the team into action. Fred scored a run, bringing their total to four before Susan again struck out.

She cringed at the memory. Definitely the weakest player on the team.

When the Morleyville catcher caught Paul's hit, marking their second out, a tense gloom had settled over the Visitor's dugout. But then Alice bunted toward third and managed to cross first base before the ball arrived. Chuck knocked a line drive that slipped past their shortstop. When the mayor got a hit, a wave of excitement swept through the dugout. Even Norman was on his feet. Or, foot. Susan glanced where he stood leaning against the dugout wall, a crutch on his right side and his toe resting on the ground.

Little Norm strutted toward home, swinging his bat. On third base, Alice bent her knees in readiness. Chuck took a few steps off second, the Morleyville shortstop watching him warily. On first, Jerry cupped his hands and called, "Out of the park, Little Norm!"

Susan glanced at the bleachers, where Daddy sat wedged between Tuesday and Wilma Rightmier. He switched his attention from the game to her, and his smile widened. When had she last seen him looking so relaxed? Her heart light, Susan turned back to the game.

In the batter's box, Little Norm stomped his feet. Puffs of dust rose to be whisked away by a light breeze. He hefted his bat into position, bounced it for balance a few times, and then jerked a nod. The Morleyville pitcher wound up and lobbed the ball. Susan's breath caught in her chest as it sailed forward.

With a swing that made hers look like a gentle tap, Little Norm's bat smacked the ball.

"Yeah!" she screamed, her voice mingling with the crowd inside the dugout and out.

Sharon leaped up beside her and the two women clung together, jumping like kids, while they watched Little Norm's hit fly past the pitcher. The Morleyville second baseman dove for it and missed. It bounced, and the Goose Creek runners took off.

Alice crossed home plate while the woman in centerfield raced after the ball.

Chuck didn't even pause as he rounded third and sprinted toward home. Jerry reached third at the same time the woman snatched up the ball and, with barely a fraction of a second's hesitation, flew down the home stretch at top speed.

Susan gasped and locked the breath in her lungs, clutching Sharon's arms, as the Morleyville player threw a long ball toward home.

"Sliiiiiiide, mayor!" Justin shouted.

Jerry slid.

The catcher caught the ball.

The umpire's call came with a swipe of his hands. "Safe."

Screeching at the top of her lungs, Susan dashed out of the dugout and catapulted toward Justin, nearly knocking him down when she slammed into him, hugging for all she was worth.

"We're tied! We're tied!"

The team's cheers as they welcomed the three runners to the dugout nearly deafened her to his answering shout. "We're tied and Little Norm's on third."

"And you're up to bat." She squeezed him again. "Knock the stuffing out of that ball."

Hers were not the only high spirits as Justin strode to the batter's box. Though she may have been the only one to think him the most breathtakingly handsome man on either team, everyone agreed that he was the most capable when it came to softball.

"We've got this." Jerry's comment exuded confidence as they watched Justin take his stance.

Silence fell over the park, teams and onlookers alike, and the sound of Justin's bat pounding the base thudded like a woodpecker on a log. He placed his feet, shuffled his weight. The pitch sailed toward him, completing its arc at exactly the right spot. He swung. The ball flew toward left field at knee-level, skipping across the grass like a smooth stone on a lake.

Little Norm plowed down the home stretch and stomped on home plate, his run accompanied by cheers.

Her attention riveted on Justin, Susan could barely breathe. She wasn't entirely certain, but her heart may have stopped while she watched her boyfriend run, arms pumping. He stomped on first as he raced by. The ball, scooped up by the right fielder, was thrown to the shortstop, who tossed it to second.

Justin's shoes skidded on the chalk line as he retreated. The first baseman lifted a glove and caught the ball, and then raced forward. Susan gasped. He was trapped. Again changing directions, Justin attempted a dash forward but the second baseman stood two feet in front of him. The ball was thrown, caught, and Justin tagged.

"Out," called the umpire.

A communal groan sounded from every Goose Creek throat. The field emptied of yellow shirts as the players headed for their dugout for their last time at bat.

Drooping, Justin jogged toward his team, mumbling as he passed the mayor, "Sorry, coach."

"It's okay." Jerry slapped him on the back. "You batted in a run. We're up by one."

Heart aching for him, Susan fell in beside Justin as they entered the dugout to retrieve their gloves. "It was a good hit."

"Yeah." He forced a smile, she suspected for her benefit. "Now we've just got to hold them."

✳

Al paced in front of the dugout, sweat rolling down his back beneath the giant T-shirt and his blood pressure buzzing in his ears. This game was too stressful for an almost-retired man like him. He paused to look up at Millie, who was handing out cookies to the Wainright girls. The boys stood at the fence, their fingers hooked through the chain link, shouting encouragement to their mother and the other Goose Creek players.

If he had a heart attack, she'd feel responsible since she'd volunteered him. What a terrible burden, to live out her days knowing she'd killed her husband. He owed it to his wife to calm down and not drop dead or collapse from heat exhaustion. He dropped a towel into the icy water in the team cooler, wrung it out, and draped it across the back of his neck.

"Think I could have one of those?" Thacker pointed toward the cooler. "It's a real scorcher out here."

If anyone had earned a bottle of water today, it was Goose Creek's resident spy. Their secret weapon, Thacker's analysis, had provided enough inside information that they'd been able to hold the Morleyville team to eight runs and even managed to get two outs in this final half of the last inning. Al retrieved one and tossed it to the man. He might even be able to forgive him for the desecration of his camelias.

"Time out."

Jerry made the call and then motioned for Al and Thacker to join a consultation in the infield. Al filled his arms with water bottles and trotted across the field.

"Okay, this is it, folks," Jerry said when they were clustered around the pitcher's mound. "We're up by one run with two outs. If we get one more out, we win. If they score two, we lose." He gestured toward Thacker's report. "What's the deal on this gal coming up to bat?"

Thacker shuffled through his papers. "She's a leftie. Batting average of four hundred since I started tracking her."

Little Norm looked over the tops of their heads at the woman swinging a bat in the on-deck circle. "That's not so great."

"No, but she's hitting well today." Thacker waggled an eyebrow at the big pitcher. "She's gotten two hits off of you, buddy."

Little Norm bristled but remained silent.

"A leftie, huh?" Justin raised his gaze from the paper to Jerry. "That means it's coming toward you."

"Unless she pops a good one," the mayor answered. "Then it's going to left field."

Every head turned. The veterinarian stood in left field surrounded by a wide, empty area. Using her glove as a fan, she waved it in front of her face. Nobody needed to voice the obvious. So far, she had struck out every time at bat and fielded one hit too late to tag the runner.

Jerry faced the pitcher. "You've got to strike this batter out."

"Listen, Norm," Justin said, "you probably know this already, but it's harder to hit a pitch breaking away from you."

Judging from the blank expression that crept over Little Norm's face, the man had no more idea what Justin was talking about than Al did. And that was zero.

"What I mean is this." Justin raised his hands to demonstrate. "If the ball coming toward a batter curves in at the last minute, the batter can see it. But if it breaks the other way…"

Though Little Norm watched Justin closely, his face paled.

Justin put on a smile that looked a little forced. "Never mind. You've been awesome all day. Just do your best."

The big man threw his chest out. "No problem."

Justin slapped him on the shoulder and the meeting broke. Striding back toward the dugout, Al used the end of his towel to wipe his face.

"We're going to do it." Thacker fanned himself with his report. "I've got a feeling."

Glancing toward Susan in left field, Al had a feeling too. And it wasn't a good one.

✻

Susan watched the conference on the pitcher's mound. When all eight faces turned her way, a tight fist of panic clenched in her chest. Why were they staring at her?

The discussion ended and her teammates spread out across the infield. As Justin strode toward the baseline, he caught and held her gaze. Was he trying to tell her something? He arrived at the shortstop position and, still looking her way, held his glove up in front of his body with both hands. She knew that signal. Whenever they practiced, that's how he'd instructed her to ready herself. He was sending her a warning to be ready.

Her throat squeezed shut.

So far her prayers had been answered. Only one ball had come her way all day. Well, a few had been hit in this direction, but low enough or short enough for the mayor to catch them. All she'd had to do was stand here, perspiring in the sun, and watch her teammates play. Except for the few disastrous turns at bat, this was exactly what she'd hoped for.

*Why did I ever agree to do this?*

Sure, it was fun hanging out in the dugout and cheering on the team. But playing was a far cry from fun.

A woman from Morleyville stepped into the chalk box around home plate. A few feet behind her, Fred squatted on his haunches and raised his mitt to the ready position.

The lump in Susan's throat might be her heart. Though she knew that to be a physical impossibility, what else could that throbbing mass blocking her windpipe be? She glanced toward the stands where Daddy and the rest of the Goose Creek fans stood in the bleachers. He bent down slightly when Tuesday said something to him, and then nodded, his attention on the woman at bat.

Little Norm's first pitch went wide. Fred had to scurry sideways to catch it.

"Ball one." The umpire's voice barely reached to this distance.

Justin called, "It's all right, Norm. Shake it off."

He did, literally, waving his hands at his sides and rolling his shoulders before he caught the ball thrown to him by Fred. He tossed the ball from his hand to his glove a few times before setting his feet on the mound.

Though Susan detected no difference at all between his first attempt and his second, that time the pitch flew straight toward Fred's mitt. The woman's bat met the ball. *Thwak!*

The ball soared high.

The player dropped her bat and sprinted for first.

Justin's voice sounded in her head. *Just watch the ball...*

She watched. The ball arced, a white spot against a deep blue sky, and then began its descent. Her pulse thudding in her ears, Susan realized it was heading toward left field. Toward her.

*...put yourself beneath it...*

Head thrown back, she ran a few steps forward. Then to her right. No, too far. Or maybe not. For cryin' out loud, how was she supposed to know where the stupid thing would land?

*...and let it fall into your glove.*

Hands held high, she planted her feet, opened her glove, and closed her eyes.

And felt a solid impact as the ball dropped into her glove.

Cheers from the crowd penetrated the ringing in her ears. She'd caught it! Lowering her glove, she peered inside, just to be sure. Like an oversized egg, the softball rested in a nest of leather.

Running toward the infield, Susan stretched her legs as if she were competing in the fifty-yard dash. Justin met her at the edge of the grass and swept her into his arms.

"You did it!" He whirled her around. "You won the game."

Susan found herself the center of a crowd of maroon-clad players, all of them hugging her and each other, laughing and shouting and thumping her on the back. Over Alice's shoulder she spied Jerry strutting across the field toward the Morleyville mayor, his chest puffed out like an overinflated balloon.

Somehow she was swept across the infield, surrounded by cheering people. Where was Justin? In all the excitement she'd lost sight of him. She looked around and spied him ahead, standing at the fence behind home plate and talking with...

Daddy?

Her father handed something to Justin, and then looked up at her. An unreadable emotion clouded his features for an instant, and then a wide grin spread across his face.

Beaming, he clapped his hands and shouted, "I'm proud of you!"

Happy tears blurred her vision. What better praise could a daughter hope for?

And then Justin was once again at her side, grabbing her hand and tugging her forward. "Come here, Suz."

"Where?"

"Just over here."

He pulled her across the dry, dusty field and then turned. With a hand on her arm, he adjusted her position. "There."

Looking down, she realized she stood inside the chalk-drawn batter's box. She raised a questioning gaze to his face.

Holding her eyes with a steady gaze, Justin knelt before her. One knee dropped onto home plate. A sudden silence fell, both on the field and off, so that his words rang clearly across the field.

"Susan Jeffries, will you marry me?"

# Chapter Eighteen

If attendance at the ballgame had been impressive, the crowd gathered around the Goose Creek water tower was nothing short of extraordinary. Millie kept a tight grip on Albert's arm as they left their car parked on Maple Avenue and joined a steady stream of Creekers trickling toward the crowd. When he would have plunged into the multitude, she pulled him to a stop.

"Don't you think we'll have a better view from back here?"

Craning his neck, he squinted upward. "Let's go around to the other side so the sun's not in our eyes."

A good plan. They edged around the throng to the opposite side, where the sun beat on their backs instead of their faces. She inspected the crown of Albert's head, where his hair was thinning even more rapidly than on top. Why hadn't she insisted he wear a hat?

Most everyone here was familiar to her. Well, and why wouldn't they be? She'd lived among them for over half her life. She exchanged a smile with Frieda and Betty. Just beyond them Mrs. Easterly hugged her fluffy Maltese, Precious.

"Here's Millie," said a voice behind her. "Maybe she knows something."

Turning, she found Doris Pulliam and Nina Baker edging between people to approach her and Albert.

"About what?" she asked.

"The new spa that's coming to town." Excitement sparked in Doris's eyes. "It'll open before the fall festival, I heard."

"A spa?"

Nina nodded. "A day spa. Ernie heard it from someone at church. It'll have facials and manicures and aromatherapy."

"Imagine, a day spa in Goose Creek." Doris smiled broadly. "I can't wait to make an appointment."

"Me too," agreed Nina. "I heard they'll offer massages, too. I'll be first in line for that."

Massage? Puzzle pieces fell into place. "I might have heard a whisper or two about that. What's the name going to be?"

"Ernie said something about Tuesday." Nina's brow wrinkled. "But he must have gotten that wrong. A spa wouldn't just be open on Tuesdays, would it?"

Millie agreed on the unlikelihood of any business being open only one day a week. She faced the tower. Good for Tuesday Love. She might make a go of her business after all.

Al pointed across the heads of the onlookers. "Looks like they're about to start."

The sturdy figure of Sandra Barnes ascended the metal ladder. Millie watched her progress, breath shallow as the woman climbed high above the watchers. She reached the top and disappeared in an opening in the platform high above. The walkway had been covered for weeks with scaffolding and canvas, which now hid the painter as well as the tower's barrel.

Little Norm followed, climbing with a sure step. Not until he also disappeared from view did Millie let out a breath. Thank goodness they both had better balance than poor, curious Junior.

"Good afternoon, folks." A familiar voice, artificially magnified, drew her attention once again to the ground. Mayor Selbo stood beside one of the tower's support legs, the top of his head barely visible. He waved a white megaphone in the air. "Some of you probably can't see me. Sorry about that, but there's no way I'm climbing up there with those two."

Millie and Albert joined their neighbors' laughter.

"Let me begin by thanking you all for your patience and support."

"He isn't going to give a political speech, is he?" Al grumbled. "It's hot out here."

Millie squeezed his hand, which was damp with perspiration. As Jerry launched into a list of those who had been instrumental in securing the Southern painter for the task of creating a piece of art that would make Goose Creek proud, she scanned the crowd.

"There's Susan and Justin." She pointed out the couple, who were paying scant attention to the mayor but were engaged primarily in gazing into each other's eyes. Nearby stood Thomas, his expression a little strained, in Millie's opinion. But at least he wasn't scowling.

Jerry appeared to be wrapping up his speech. "But I know you didn't come out this evening to hear me talk."

"He's got that right," Al said, and several heads in their vicinity nodded.

"I asked Ms. Barnes if she'd like to say a few words," Jerry announced, "but she'd rather let her work speak for her. So let's take a look, shall we?" The megaphone pointed upward toward the tower. "Ready when you are."

Millie squeezed Albert's hand. "This is so exciting."

An opening appeared in the canvas, and a tantalizing glimpse of color peeked through. The fabric rippled and shivered for a moment as the pair apparently experienced some difficulty. Then one side dropped. Little Norm scurried around the platform and slipped behind the remaining curtain, and a few seconds later the rest of the canvas fell.

Millie covered her mouth, astonished by intricacy of the artwork hovering over the town.

A peaceful pasture wrapped around the lower part of the barrel, gentle swells in the grass—which was a beautiful deep *green*, she noted with satisfaction—giving the impression of stretching far into the distance to a misty horizon. Sunlight sparkled on a narrow stream, where a goose and six fuzzy goslings splashed in the shallows. Across an azure blue sky flew a flock of geese in V-formation beneath ornate lettering that proudly proclaimed, *Goose Creek, Ke*—

Well, that was all Millie could see from this vantage point, but presumably the word continued around the other side.

An admiring gasp rose from the watchers. For one moment everyone stood with their heads thrown back, soaking in the beauty of the town's new icon. As one, thunderous applause rose toward the pair on the tower, who raised their fists in victory.

❈

Al turned off the street and navigated the car up the cracked driveway. One blinding sliver of sun showed above the western horizon, and the suffocating temperature had finally cooled to a tolerable level. The day's excitement had taken its toll on him, and he looked forward to bedtime more than any day in recent memory.

Millie twisted sideways in the passenger seat. "I did something you don't know about."

If he weren't so tired he might feel some alarm. "Can it wait until tomorrow?"

"No, it can't. Please stop the car in the front."

When his wife had something rolling around in that lovely head of hers, any resistance on his part was a wasted effort. Resigned, he steered around the semicircle and came to a halt beside the front porch. When the engine had been shut off and the keys removed, he faced her. "Okay, out with it."

Her eyes moved as she searched his face. "You know I love you, don't you, Albert?"

Uh-oh. This could be serious.

"And I love you," he assured her.

"When we bought this house, I really thought you'd come to love it like I do." Her hands clutched the seatbelt, which stretched across her shoulder. "I'm sorry. That was selfish of me."

In the decades since their wedding, apologies had become a necessary part of their marital language. He'd grown used to them. But this one felt deeper than the simple, "I'm sorry," when she shrank his favorite sweater in the laundry.

"We're together. That's all that matters." He reached for her hand. "I mean that."

A soft smile curved the lips he had loved to kiss for more years than he could remember. "Thank you." Then a dimple punctuated each cheek. "Let's go inside."

Together they climbed the steps and entered the house. Rufus charged down the hall, toenails clacking on the hardwood and his bark echoing up the stairs.

"It's us, you dimwit." Al bent to assure the creature with an affectionate pat.

"Come on." Millie tugged on his arm, pulling him down the hallway, through the dining room, and out the French doors onto the verandah.

Rufus raced ahead of them into the yard, once again barking with fury, and startled a pair of squirrels who leaped off the birdfeeders and made a dash to the safety of the trees. Okay, maybe not such a dimwit after all.

Drawing him to the edge of the porch, she turned with a wide grin. "What do you think?"

"About?" He looked up. The yard stretched before him, peaceful in the rapidly diminishing light. A pair of Canada geese settled at the edge of the cattails beyond the pond, its surface glassy in the still evening air. The swing in the gazebo—

Wait. Circling the gazebo was a row of shrubs that had not been there this morning. Even in the dim light he recognized the shape of the greenery.

"Camelias."

He dropped her hand and left the porch, hurrying across the grass to inspect the shrubs. Blooms gone at this time of year, but camelias without a doubt.

He whirled toward his wife. "You bought me camelias."

But she shook her head. "I didn't buy them. I rescued them."

Her meaning dawned on him, and he turned once again to the plants. "Do you mean these are *my* camelias?"

Grinning, she nodded. "I called Franklin and asked him to save them. The Wainright boys helped with the planting this morning while you were at the ballgame." A delightful laugh erupted from her. "Do you like my surprise?"

He did not know enough words to express his feelings. Instead, he enfolded her in an embrace and nuzzled her neck with a kiss that made her giggle like a girl.

Standing there with the light disappearing and the frogs in the pond beginning their nightly serenade, Al relished the feel of his wife's arms around him. Where was home, if not right here?

"Albert, look." She turned in his embrace and pointed at the sky. "Fireworks."

An explosion of fiery color blossomed in the night sky. Resting his chin on his wife's head, Al watched the sparks fizzle, only to be replaced by a new and brighter burst.

Suddenly Millie stiffened. She stepped away and turned a wide-eyed look on him. "I think Violet's rubbing off on me. The fireworks reminded me of Susan and Justin, and I thought, *out with the old, in with the new.*" A hand rose to cover her mouth. "You don't think we're old and on our way out, do you?"

Al adopted a wolfish grin. "Come here, Mildred Richardson, and let me show you a thing or two about fireworks."

He hooked her waist with an arm, pulled her to him, and smothered her giggle with his kiss.

# Acknowledgments

I always approach writing the second (and third, and fourth) book in a series with a touch of apprehension, and *Renovating the Richardsons* was no exception. Will the characters I fell in love with in *The Most Famous Illegal Goose Creek Parade* be as appealing in their continuing roles? If new readers pick this book up first, will they be as entranced by Goose Creek as those who visited my fictional town in the previous stories? In the opinion of my first readers (who include my mother, so maybe they're not exactly impartial), the answer is, "Yes!" When you've turned the last page, I hope you'll agree.

Once again, I'm grateful to a lot of people for helping me tell this story. First, to my brainstorming team, Anna Zogg and Marilynn Rockelman, both incredible brainstorming partners and talented authors themselves. I do not exaggerate when I say that without them, this book wouldn't have been nearly as much fun to write or to read. Thanks also to my mom, Amy Barkman, for helping me clean up the first draft and for providing a never-ending source of encouragement.

I deeply appreciate Jerry and Cindie Selbo (the real ones, not their fictitious namesakes) for allowing me to use their names in the Goose Creek series. Even though the characters who bear their names are completely fictional, it takes a certain amount of trust and courage to let someone use your name in a book. Most of all, I treasure their friendship.

I've had the pleasure of knowing two incredibly skilled massage therapists for many years. Shawn Galloway and Susan Ashley have provided me with countless hours of muscle therapy and relaxation that enabled me to write the massage sections believably. And I appreciate Linda Fugate, my insurance agent, for helping me figure out what would typically be covered when Millie and Al found mold and squirrels in their house.

Thanks to my agent, Wendy Lawton, for being my professional champion and my personal friend.

I'm truly fortunate to work with the talented folks at Harvest House Publishers. I hesitate to mention names because I'm so aware that there's an entire team of people with whom I never interact who have worked hard to make this book the best it can be. I am so thankful for you! I do want to thank Jeff Marion, who has been my contact regarding the covers for this series. (Aren't they delightful?!) And especially my tremendous editor, Kathleen Kerr. Her skill and professionalism have been the subject of countless prayers of gratitude. Kathleen, when you see this book in its final form, go indulge yourself with your favorite form of chocolate. You deserve it.

My husband, Ted Smith, deserves some sort of medal for putting up with me when I have a book in my head that I'm trying to get down on paper. Ted, thank you. How could I write about happy marriages without you, my role model?

Most of all, thank you to Jesus, the Source of true creativity that flows like a never-ending river.

And thank *you,* dear reader, for accompanying me on another trip to Goose Creek. Do me a favor, would you? Drop me a note and tell me what you think of the book. You can find me online at www.virginiasmith.org or on Facebook at www.facebook.com/ginny.p.smith.

# About the Author

Virginia Smith is the author of more than two dozen inspirational novels and 50 articles and short stories. Her fondness for cats took on new meaning during the writing of this book, when she discovered a litter of feral kittens living beneath her gazebo. Now registered with her local humane society as an official foster mom to homeless cats, Ginny finds immense satisfaction in nursing newborn and sick kittens back to health to prepare them for their forever homes. She lives less than ten miles from the small town that is the real-life inspiration for Goose Creek. An avid reader with eclectic tastes in fiction, Ginny writes in a variety of styles, from lighthearted relationship stories to breath-snatching suspense. Visit her website to find out more about her and her books. www.VirginiaSmith.org.

Don't miss the rest of the story!

In this first book of the Tales from the Goose Creek B&B, you'll fall in love with a small town that feels like coming home. Its quirky characters and their many shenanigans will make you laugh out loud as they touch a place in your heart.

Even though retirement is still three years away, Al Richardson is counting the days. He anticipates many enjoyable years in which every day feels like Saturday. But Al's wife, Millie, has different plans for their retirement. When she learns that a Victorian-era home is up for sale, Millie launches a full-blown campaign to convince Al that God's plan for them is to turn that house into a B&B.

But a B&B won't be the only change for the small Kentucky town. A new veterinarian has hung up her shingle, but she's only got one patient—the smelly dog belonging to her part-time receptionist. And sides are being taken in the issue of the water tower, which needs a new coat of paint...but no one can agree who should paint it.

The situation is coming to a head. Who could have imagined a town protest over a water tower? And who would believe it could culminate in an illegal parade?

Get lost in a novel that reminds you why you love reading.

*Bonus!*

This bonus e-only short story is the perfect introduction to Goose Creek. Set in the years before the Richardsons launch their bed and breakfast scheme, the quirky residents of the small Kentucky town are all in a tizzy over the upcoming Fall Festival. Alison, Al and Millie's headstrong daughter, astounds everyone with the news that she's getting married—in three weeks—to a Colombian! As her parents frantically try to stop the nuptials, Dr. Horatio, Goose Creek's beloved veterinarian, is determined to solve the mystery of the six-toed kittens that have been popping up all over town.

To learn more about Harvest House books and
to read sample chapters, visit our website:

**www.harvesthousepublishers.com**

HARVEST HOUSE PUBLISHERS
EUGENE, OREGON